Stumbled Upon Destiny

A Star-Crossed Knot

I0666891

Stumbled Upon Destiny

A Star-Crossed Knot

Jolsna Rajan

Srishti
PUBLISHERS & DISTRIBUTORS

Srishti Publishers & Distributors
N-16, C. R. Park
New Delhi 110 019
editorial@srishtipublishers.com

First published by
Srishti Publishers & Distributors in 2013

Copyright © Jolsna Rajan, 2013

Typeset by EGP at Srishti

Dedication

I would like to dedicate my first book to my parents M.Rajan and Girija Rajan whose guidance has always been quiet and assured. The subject of the book is very different and unrelated to my parents but I would not have been able to write a full length novel without their huge support in life...

ACKNOWLEDGEMENT

I would like to extend heartfelt thanks to my colleague and friend Shyam Nair without whom I could not have completed my story, 'Stumbled Upon Destiny'. He has always been a great guide in all my work. The time we spent in discussing our stories, and what they meant to us has always been an inspiration to write. He has also helped me in editing every chapter of this book. I am currently co-authoring another story with him and would like to thank him for all his support.

And, in no particular order, I would like to thank Seena, Hariprasad, Rakshith, Mandira, Suday, Archana, Suraj, Ranjith Nair and Manjula for being there always.

PREFACE

'Stumbled Upon Destiny' is an 'every family' story, inspired by common people around.

The story is about a 'modern arranged marriage', an outcome of parental pressure. Things begin with a couple whose ideologies and expectations are as different as chalk and cheese being forced to live together under the same roof. From then it is all downhill, often culminating in a divorce, that an all-so-common ailment afflicting many marriages in the modern times.

Meera Madhav and Vineet Hariharan are two such persons brought together after much deliberation by the elders in their respective families. However, nobody bothers to check if the two people in question are actually right for each other. Abstract concepts like 'chemistry' and 'wavelength' are beyond the comprehension of these elders who are busy dealing with even more abstract concepts such as stars and horoscopes.

The couple live together, fight with each other and make all the mistakes that young and incompatible people are likely to make, while maintaining a façade of bliss for the benefit of the rest of the world. And like many other couples, they eventually lose the will to carry on the charade and decide to call their marriage off. Their story ends. Should they have called it off? Is the idea of an arranged marriage that bad?

I have attempted to bring in people of various ages, their

thoughts and temperaments. I strongly believe that every reader would be able to relate to the characters at some point of the story. My protagonists, Meera and Vineet belong to a place called Palakkad in Kerala. So a few Malayalam words used in the story, Acha (Father), Chechi (Sister), Achamma (Grandmother) being some of them. My intention has been only to give my readers the opportunity to savour the unique flavours of a Malayali Brahmin family.

Another said – *"Why, ne'er a peevish Boy, would break the bowl from which he drank in Joy; Shall He that made the Vessel in pure Love And Fancy, in an after Rage destroy!"*

– from the *Rubaiyat of Omar Khayyam*

Part 1 - Vineet

PROLOGUE

Were things between us really that bad? Maybe they were. What else would you call a marriage that leaves no good memories!

We could have worked things out. I knew that at least I could have.

But she never wanted it to work out!

Who was I kidding? It had been over even before it had started. Maybe that is the definition of the 'modern-day-arranged-marriage'. Something that is over much before it has even started. A marriage that never works.

Madhu was right. You need to fall in love to get married. It can never be the other way round.

I had never imagined, even in my worst nightmare, that I would see this day in my life.

THE DIVORCE

"Are we fine, Vineet?"

Was I fine?

"Yes, Deepak. I don't have any second thoughts about it. I am sure Meera thinks the same." I had never been in Deepak's office before, always preferring to meet my friend outside. Deepak was a buddy from school and now a divorce lawyer. My eyes took in the depressing walls, lined with rack after rack of depressing books. Everything in that office seemed to reflect the depressing work that was carried on its confines. I wondered if anyone ever thanked Deepak when he helped them win their 'freedom' from a lifetime of pain. Something told me that the curses he was same to leave accumulated over the years would have far outweigh the occasional expression of gratitude that might strayed his way. No wonder, that the walls of his office looked so dank and miserable!

"Deepak, your office gives me the creeps, man. You should seriously think of improving the interiors. No, actually, I think you should just change your profession to something better, like a legal consultant in a company or something. Anything but a divorce lawyer, man! Depression seems to be literally hanging from your walls...actually peeling off it in some places, I must add."

That was what had prompted Deepak to ask me if I was fine.

I was fine. I didn't have an option, really, other than to be fine. I, Vineet Hariharan, was splitting with Meera Madhav, my wife of nearly a year. And Deepak was the man taking care of the legal formalities. The previous evening, I had met Deepak over a cup of coffee. "I was wrong, Deepak. Now I know how people feel when they are going through a separation. They just want to get rid of it as quickly and painlessly as possible."

While Deepak was running through a couple of issues with his staff, I stepped out. His office was in a building full of other lawyers' offices. I sat on a bench just outside the door. The corridor was teeming with people who were sailing in the same boat. Most of them were older than me. Perhaps it made sense for people to walk out of unhappy marriages after having given it a good five or ten years. In comparison, I had hardly given my marriage any time. That I was the rookie among these tried and tested veterans of wedlock was there for all to see. Especially to that seventy-something woman who was sitting on a bench across the corridor with her son. She kept looking at me with sad eyes and I had to ultimately look away.

Deepak came out of his office eventually. "Vineet, this one is taking a little long. Another twenty minutes or so." Since I was in no particular hurry, I decided to make the best use of time and get photocopies of the documents.

Meera's yellow Alto entered the compound and brushed past me on its way to the parking lot. A couple of minutes later, she came into view, walking towards the building with her uncle in tow. I was seeing her after months.

Meera Madhav, my soon not-to-be, if there is such a phrase as that, had called off our marriage within a few months of our being together. After initially going through a spate of emotions, ranging between surprise, shock, sadness and anger, all in good measure, I had finally come to terms with her decision. I now realized that it was all for the best. We were a mismatched couple, who were better off without each other.

She was initially a very difficult person to be with, unpredictable to the extreme. I was never sure of what the right thing to say to her was. Seeing the yellow Alto after so long had triggered off some unpleasant memories.

"Why would anyone buy a yellow car?" This casual remark of mine had triggered off a bitter response. Her reaction had been borderline scary! After a sharp retort, she had lapsed into a cold silence, almost immediately I recalled. I had sworn to myself never to question Meera ever again. Silence, as they say, is one of the main ingredients of a successful marriage. Why had mine gone wrong then?

I had actually started accepting her and her ways. All that unpredictability apart, she was really a good person. My parents loved her. The only reason my neighbours continued to believe that she was the daughter-in-law and not the daughter of the house was because they had actually seen me growing up in the neighbourhood!

Perhaps, it had all been simply too good to last. The truth was that we were as apart as chalk and cheese. And communication, the cornerstone of all successful marriages, was conspicuous by its absence in ours. Why had my parents liked her so much?

"Lost in thoughts, Vineet?" Deepak had come outside looking for me.

"Not really. Just reiterating to myself why I have no regrets."

Deepak and I went in. Meera and Vittal uncle were in the corridor. Vittal uncle was looking grumpier than usual. Of this I could not be certain because that was the only expression he ever gave me. I had learnt to gauge his moods by the varying degrees of grumpiness. I had once seen a smiling photo of the man in Meera's family album and wondered if he had a more pleasant, identical twin!

Meera smiled at me. I wondered if she had had second

thoughts. But the hope faded as quickly as it had come when she stepped into the office without even bothering to enquire about my well being, in spite of having met me after ages.

Meera was wearing her glasses. She only wore her glasses when she was upset. Was all this upsetting her? Well, it must have. Both of us had every reason to be upset.

We sat in the little reception area in Deepak's office, while Deepak and Vittal uncle excused themselves for a few minutes. I was not sure whether to strike a conversation with Meera or not. Every time I glanced at her, she seemed to be looking away. After a few minutes of this awkwardness, I gathered the courage to say something. But even as I turned to her, Meera got up from her chair and walked away answering a call, leaving me looking like a fool, with my mouth hanging open. So much for my attempts at communication!

I had met her for the first time at her house…a meeting that had the blessings of both our families. We were talking to each other in her room. I was so embarrassed that my questions kept coming out all wrong. "So, you are a sales executive!" As a software engineer, I had been so caught up in my own profession that I had failed to keep myself abreast of the various fancy designations that companies dish out to their employees. So, to me, it had seemed like a perfectly harmless question.

"I am a sales account manager." The response had been sharp and I could have sworn that icicles dripped from her voice when she hammered my misconception out.

Vittal uncle and Deepak walked in with a set of documents each. I made one more, feeble attempt at smiling at the man. The smile died before reaching him because Vittal uncle shot it down with a pair of glaring eyes that most resembled a smoking double-barrelled gun! Vittal uncle was a thin man who could be mistaken for a person who had never had the privilege of having seen a reasonably filled plate of food in his life. It was only after I had gotten to know him better that I realized that he had the appetite of a four-member family and their dog put together. The dog analogy was the result of once watching him chew a particularly resistant piece of drumstick just as I had seen my neighbour's dog chewing its bone. Vittal uncle had never liked me and, pardon the pun, made no bones about it. On the day of the wedding, Meera's dad had drawn me aside and spoken in a quiet voice about how his daughter was from then on my responsibility and how I was supposed to take care of her. Hardly had he turned away than Vittal uncle popped up and let me know in no uncertain terms that I was supposed to take care of his daughter as well. For a rather illogical moment, I wondered if this was some kind of package deal, where I got to walk away with his daughter also. He had, of course, been talking about Meera, who, I was soon to realize, was no less than a daughter to him. And the feeling was mutual. Meera even called Vittal uncle, *acha*, which in Malayalam means father.

Meera's family was great to be with. I had always liked visiting them, but rarely got the chance. Meera chose to visit them mostly on her own. As luck would have had it, Vittal uncle would always be present on the few occasions that I did get to visit my in-laws. The man would bombard me with a set of uncomfortable questions and I would unerringly give him all the wrong answers. I would realize I had failed in the quiz only when foster father and foster daughter would walk out of the room like a set of perfectly synchronized ballet dancers.

"Meera, Vineet, we have a few things to clarify. Shall we begin with you, Meera?" Deepak was asking her about the final decision when I noticed that she was carrying her laptop. She was going back to work! Why was I even surprised!

I knew her final decision. For once, we were agreeing upon something!

NO TIME TO RECOUP

"I don't see why we should go through this over and over again, Deepak. I am tired of having to clarify myself every time." We were done with the so called discussion for the day. I walked out with Deepak a little while after Meera and her uncle had left the office. I was irritated with the entire process and also with Deepak. I had always had my reservations about lawyers, courts and their proceedings. Some dude making an allegation, some other dude countering it and a third altogether unconnected dude sitting and passing judgment on it all. It is bad enough to screw things up but then having to stand up in front of many pairs of accusing eyes and justifying oneself was altogether a trying affair. And like most people, I had thought that this would never happen to me!

"Deepak, I don't like it that Meera and her folks have to go through this every time. Both of us have agreed to a mutual divorce. For the final time, I want you to get that, ok?" I could afford to vent out a bit of my frustration on a childhood buddy, I figured.

At the office, Deepak pored through the entire document once more. Considering that it was nothing more than a slightly modified version of an extremely standard document, I wondered why he was going through all that trouble. Eventually, he appeared to be satisfied with the content and the document was through. Our concluding opinions had been taken into account and the next time we were to meet would be our last time as husband and wife. They had taken our final opinions. That there were hardly any accusations leveled was a relief to me. Meera had put her foot down on not wanting any alimony, much to the disbelief of lawyers on either side.

"Vineet, you need a smoke. Here, light one." Deepak was trying to calm me down, but it was not going to help.

"Vineet, you don't need to feel very worried for Meera. Remember, when her lawyer raked up that charge of you having an affair with another woman? Did she even object? So what do you call a woman who sees red every time you talk to a female colleague? Broadminded? I know I'm talking about your wife, man. But I simply could not stop myself." Deepak had a point, I thought. Why was I even being bothered about a girl who had not had a second thought before cutting me to pieces in front of my father!

That incident was burnt deep into my memory. Dad had accompanied me to Deepak's office that day. Meera had come in with her father and lawyer. Her lawyer was a cock-eyed, devil of a feminist, who seemed hell bent on having us separated. She read out from the document she had drafted. I could have sworn that the woman was smacking her lips when she came to the juiciest part. *"My client states that whereas she has been nothing but a faithful wife to the said Mr. Vineet Hariharan, he has not reciprocated in the same manner. He has had an illicit affair with one Ms. Madhurima Srivastava, a colleague of his..."* The rest of the statement was a blur. While I visibly balked at the accusation, dad's reaction had been more dramatic. He shot one look at me and then stormed out of the room. I followed him, but could only watch as he hailed an auto and went home. For days after words, I had tried convincing my parents that it had been nothing more than a gimmick that her lawyer had employed to lend credence to her case. I even got Deepak to call my folks and explain, but to no avail.

Deepak was right. I did not have to feel guilty. It was time to get a hold on myself and go to work. Yes, that's what I needed to do. After all, wasn't that exactly what Meera was proposing to do, carrying her laptop and all to the hearing? Why should I be the emotional fool then? My divorce was not going to stop the world from spinning around or something. Two minutes later, therefore, I was in my car, driving off to work.

I was beginning to feel better once I was in the car. Earlier, I had been too agitated to notice that Deepak had smoked away my entire cigarette. I lit another one and had hardly taken a puff, when my phone rang.

"Hi, *Ma.*"

"What happened Vineet? Is everything over? You did not even call us to let us know. We were worried, Vineet. You don't even think about us. Are you even going to tell us about it?"

For a fleeting second, I had visions of myself as a call center employee and my mom as a dissatisfied customer. If my employers had recorded the conversation we had just had and studied it for quality and monitoring purposes, they would surely have used it to train fresh recruits on how to retain their composure in the face of a barrage of questions from an irate customer. Given the situation, I think I did a remarkable job of keeping the irritation out of my voice.

"*Ma*, another six months."

"Six months! Deepak told me that it will be over soon and he will take care of it. Let me call him up. Did he make you stand at the podium in the court? Was there a judge? Were there many people?" Even as I recovered from this fresh onslaught of questions, I realized that they had been prompted by the movies of her generation. All court scenes in these movies had been liberally laced with blade dialogs like "Yes, your honour", "Objection, M'lord", and "Objection overruled". My poor mom believed that court proceedings were carried out exactly in that exaggerated fashion to this day.

"*Ma*, didn't papa tell you about it. Maybe you can ask him now. I know he is on the other line." I always hated it when papa picked the other line when I was speaking to mom.

"Vineet, stop it. He did tell me about it, but how do you expect him to be an expert on these matters? Have we had a single divorce in the family before? I did not tell you this earlier, but Susheela aunty has called four times since yesterday asking me about it. She kept on saying how shocked she was that Vineet, the ideal boy in the entire family, could end up with a divorce." I heard a distinct sniff at the other end, meaning that mom was now preparing to move into the sobbing stage.

"*Ma*, I am upset and the last thing I want is you to nag me. Instead of bothering about me, Susheela aunty should worry about her son who is loafing around without a job for six months now."

"*Kanna*, don't say that. She likes you and cares for you. I know you feel the same." Her sobs were now steadily picking strength.

"Yeah, *Ma*. I am sorry ok. You take care. I am driving and so will call you later. I will come home early, alright?"

"Really? Will you have dinner with us?" She was already feeling better. That was the best part of talking to my mom. She bounced back so quickly.

"Yes, Sulu."

"Alright, *Kanna*." Calling her Sulu made her very happy. Sulochana, her name had been nicked to Sulu by her husband, but it was her son who had taken it over, popularized it and unabashedly used it to his advantage.

"Vineet, are you smoking?"

"Bye, *Ma*." I hung up on her. *Ma* always found out if I smoked. She blamed it on the many short pauses I took during the conversation. I would really have to work on my breath control skills.

Does this guy have to see my card every day? Doesn't he know me by now? It is been four years. Same guy, same car…"

"Sir, it is you." Maadesh, our security man at office greeted me with these very words every morning. I often wondered if it was just a casual remark or whether he had taken it upon himself to keep me informed that I was really me! If he happened not to say those magic words one day, would I then wander about, lost, in the vast recesses of my office, wondering who I really was?

"Yes, Maadesh. It is me." Whatever it is, cheerful as he was, he never failed to cheer me up a bit as well.

"Sir, ID card?"

"Maadesh!"

"I can't help it, sir. It is an order from the admin. Sorry, sir." And then Maadesh indulged in another one of his idiosyncrasies. He looked at the photo on my ID and then looked at my face. Having ascertained beyond doubt that it was indeed me, he waved me in with a smart salute and a big smile. I chuckled to myself, promising that the day he insisted on a DNA test, I was quitting this company for good. But, admittedly, I was beginning to feel a lot more cheerful.

No wonder Girish envied Maadesh's job. "*No thinking required. Just stand there, scrutinize your IDs like it was all part of some CBI investigation and then wave you morons in. Even I could do that. I would still like to get paid what I currently earn, though. Then it would be the ideal job for me.*" I walked into the reception, smiling at this thought, when I ran into the man himself. As usual, the burger-sized grin was well established on his chubby face.

Like his grin, everything about Girish was about food. In his life, thus far, the man had had enough food to have sustained the population of a small country for a couple of years. He was my best friend and colleague. Needless to say, Meera hated him. But, then, she hated all my friends. I wouldn't blame her entirely on the Girish-hating bit, though, because this moron of a friend of mine had once shocked her in her own kitchen. Meera had just stepped out after a bath and run into this mountain of a man busily foraging for food in her refrigerator. The girl had recovered remarkably well, I thought, for someone who had seen her very first episode of Girish versus Food. Then the fool had overstayed his welcome and tucked away happily into most of the dinner Meera had cooked for just the two of us.

"*Macha*, I was just hoping that you would come. That Chinese restaurant next to the Nokia service center has finally opened. Let us go."

Girish sounded as if he had been invited to inaugurate the place.

"Not today, Girish. Let's have lunch at the canteen, or you could go with the rest of the gang to the place."

"Don't be a sissy, Vineet. You are coming. And what is with that sulking face of yours? '*Go out with the rest of the gang*'. Be a man." I smiled at the way Girish mimicked me. Suddenly, I was more than willing to go with him even though I did not like Chinese. I walked towards the work floor with Girish trying to explain to him why I had a problem with the Chinese ever since they had occupied Tibet. The moron retorted by saying that he was not even remotely concerned about Tibet unless there were some good restaurants there. That is what I liked about the guy. He was always in such high spirits.

I was nearly at the floor, when I saw Richard approaching. He was one of the few who were aware that I was meeting the lawyer today. I had to tell him when he refused to grant me leave, something I thought he had no business to do. The big mouth that he was, there was no doubt that he would have already discussed it with a few of his cronies in the upper management.

"Vineet, you told me that you had wanted leave. What are you doing here?" Richard had a booming voice. It sounded across the floor like a thunderclap. I had the feeling that it was just a matter of time before the entire office came to know where I had been in the morning and why.

Richard was now less than an arm's length away. He said in a voice that he thought was a conspiratorial whisper, but, which was still enough to set my eardrums vibrating! "How did it go? Come let us go out for a smoke." Richard was not sounding even remotely concerned.

"Thanks, Richard, I am good." I just wanted to go in.

I swiped my access card. Why did I feel that the entire floor was looking at me? Perhaps, Richard had already been around.

I saw my friends standing near Aman's workstation.

"So he wanted me to send her flowers. I told him that I definitely would. After all, my mother-in-law is my own, isn't she? Jacob knows very well that I am being sarcastic. He did not utter a word after that. Hehe. Ah, Vineet. See I told you that you won't be able to stay away from me even for a day." Reshma Jacob, was the happy soul of the group. Apart from Girish, that is. By a strange coincidence, both these happy-go-lucky individuals had been nicknamed 'the mouth' at various stages of their association with us. While Girish had earned his nickname due to his voracious appetite, Reshma had earned hers, thanks to her nonstop chattering. We had known each other four years, having joined the company at the same time. We had gotten close to each other during the training and I had kind of fallen for her almost immediately. But the affair died a premature death as soon as I heard that the pretty girl was married to her high school sweetheart.

"Reshma, why are you wasting everyone's time? Hey, Aman."

"Hi man," Aman, the gentle soul, replied with a gentle smile. Of all the gang members, he was the one that led the perfect life. Reshma had her mother-in-law, a wedding gift she could have done without, to grumble about. Girish, when he wasn't eating, was lamenting the fact that neither he nor his parents had been able to fix up a girl for him to settle down with. I, of course, had my world famous broken marriage to brag about. So, Aman was the only guy with nothing to complain. He led a blissful family life with his lovely wife, Nira, and lovelier daughter Pari. I couldn't help envying his perfect life, even as mine took a turn for the worse.

"Vineet, we should take a poll to see if our friends enjoy my gossip or your microchip *gyaan* better." Reshu smirked.

"I've got a thousand bucks that says I'll win, Reshu."

"Yeah, right."

Aman joined in the fun. "Hey, does anyone want to bet on the fact that precisely at one, Girish will amble in to my work station and say 'hey *Macha*, let's go grab some grub…I haven't had anything to eat since I had those bondas at half past eleven, man!'"

No one was foolish enough to take the bait. At one sharp, Girish ambled towards Aman's workstation to pull us all out to that unexplored restaurant. "Guys, where is Madhu?"

"Madhu is finishing her work off, Girish. And, by the way Vineet, Madhu is on her way to a promotion." Reshu had a wicked smile on when she divulged that bit of information.

I don't know what it was with the gang when they mentioned Madhu's name around me. They would all drop whatever that they were doing and give me looks loaded with meaning. Meera apparently suspected that something was going on between Madhu and me. It seemed that my friends had similar ideas. Thankfully, at least my friends were not planning to divorce me on that account!

As a ravenous Girish began sniffing in and around Aman's cubicle for anything edible, we saw Madhu walk in with her laptop, dragging the cables along the floor. "Hi Guys."

Madhu was an independent girl, living away from her family. Like most of us, she had a sob story to tell as well. Apparently, her father had incurred huge losses in business and had failed to repay it. She, being the eldest child in the family, had taken it upon herself to repay her father's debt. She had also taken on the responsibility of putting her brothers through college.

Madhu was short, fair and slim. She was tiny enough to walk around the office undetected, staying well hidden behind cubicle walls. Over the years, she had grown fond of Bangalore in general and the office in particular. Madhu and I could relate to each other in many ways. We had discovered a lot of common interests.

We took off for lunch. We had a busy day at work. Even the unflappable Girish had his eyes glued to his monitor. Reshu texted me to check if someone had emailed him pictures of his favorite food. Richard, as usual, walked the floor passing sharp comments.

It was close to eight when I had finished all my work. I still had the energy to go on a while longer, but I decided it was time to leave. I quickly checked the meetings lined up for the next day and then shut down for the day.

"YOU HAD A DIVORCE IN THE MORNING...
DIDN'T YOU?"

In the elevator, on my way down, I remembered my promise to mom that I would be home early. I silently cursed myself for forgetting and promised myself to key in reminders on my mobile from then on. But then, I reasoned with myself that surely *Ma* knew too well how bad I was at keeping promises.

Cigarette, cigarette. I desperately wanted one. The small shop down the road was still open and I made my way to it. Memories of the discussions at Deepak's office that morning came unbidden to the mind. "Meera, is this your final decision?" Deepak had tried to give it one last shot. I realized that I was hoping she'd say '*No*' or '*Can I take some more time?*' or '*Can I think it over again?*' But, her answer had been a very steady 'Yes' and it had broken my heart. I was glad that Deepak had asked her first. Had he asked me, I would have sounded like an emotional fool!

"Two lights." I lighted my cigarette on my way back to the parking lot.

I drove home to the sound of my favourite CD playing on my car stereo. It was a pleasure to drive on Bangalore roads at that late hour.

My parents' house had not been my home a few months back. I had been living in an apartment at Chandranagar with Meera. An apartment that now held so many painful memories that I had decided to put it up for a sale. It had been a pleasure to see her yellow Alto parked outside the building. Why she chose to park it there rather than in the basement was beyond me. A few days after Meera walked out on me, I was missing the yellow machine. The stretch where she always parked it looked bare without her car, even though there were quite a few others lined up. It was then that I decided to leave Chandranagar and move in with my parents.

The lights in the living room were on. I hoped dad would be asleep, but realized there was little chance of that at ten. As I opened the gate to park my car, I saw papa watching me from a window. He then opened the door for me. I walked past him without meeting his eye and made straight for the kitchen.

"*Ma*," I hugged her tight, forgetting entirely that she might find out I had been smoking. For once, she did not. "Go wash your hands Vineet." I quickly bolted out of the kitchen before her keen sense of smell detected even a hint of tobacco on my clothes.

"*Kanna*, what is this? You cannot come home early even once. You had a divorce in the morning, didn't you?" The way *amma* said it, it seemed like she was asking me about the *dosa* I had for breakfast in the morning! "It does not seem to have affected you one bit. We were so worried for you. Why couldn't you just take leave?" I marveled at how *amma* managed to ask so many questions in one breath, while weeping copiously at the same time! Must have been the Art of Living classes she had been attending lately.

I tried to slink out of the kitchen slowly. "How will you feel better about the divorce, if you don't share it with your mother? I am the only one who will understand you, isn't it? Where are you going, Vineet? Talk to me."

"Nothing really happened, *Ma*. Since both of us were ok with the separation, everything was smooth. Deepak says that it will be over in six months. So, technically, I am not divorced yet. And I'm fine, *Ma*." I was fast approaching the very limits of my patience.

I wondered why parents had to express their own miseries with scant regard to how vulnerable their kids might be feeling!

"Then what were you doing today?" It was clear that mom had forgotten all that I had told her that morning. Was this some form of ADD that afflicted people addicted to daily soaps on TV, I wondered. Mrs. Sulochana Hariharan had probably been thinking of Susheela aunty or her favorite TV star while I was patiently explaining to her the status of my divorce on my way to work.

"*Amma*, it was a brief discussion. They asked both of us one last time if we wanted to go ahead with the divorce. They just went over the filed documents one last time. That's all."

"Good. Atleast someone else is doing the job for us. Can't you think it over again?" I could not bring myself to tell her that it was Meera who had been driving the decision. She would never buy that. Like I said, Meera was more like a daughter to my parents and they had unhesitatingly transferred the burden of having ruined the marriage to my shoulders. All my attempts to convince them otherwise had fallen on deaf ears. Papa was very agitated when he told me that "You must be wrong. It can never be, Meera." I was not going to make the mistake again of blaming her.

"No *Ma*. There is nothing to reconsider." I walked off, listening to *umma* sob again. I did not turn around to look at her. I knew that in five minutes she would be all right as the serial '*Maha Prabhu*' was about to begin. She would then be more worried about Pushpalatha, the reigning tragedy queen of the Malayalam serial industry, and the string of misfortunes that was sure to descend upon her, thanks to the twisted mind of some scriptwriter. For about half an hour, her son's divorce would be the last thing on her mind. I envied her simplicity.

I was tired. I wanted to sleep. It had been a day of speculations, work, and heartache. It was coming to an end.

NIGHT OUT WITH GIRISH

"Vineet, the meeting is at eleven. The new project is driving me up the wall. They want you to co-lead as well."

"Yes Sudanshu. But do brief me before the meeting, please."

"I will darling."

People who were not used to Sudanshu's effeminate ways would have been shocked to hear him address me thus. But that was Sudanshu for you! A woman trapped in a man's body and my immediate boss at work. He flitted from one cubicle to the other, speaking to the girls about girly accessories with perfect ease. I still remember distinctly the day he came up to Reshu, took one look at her nail polish and said, "This is *Cremosa Intense Nude*, isn't it? I had picked this up for a friend. Try the *Verniz & Cor.*" He sashayed down the passage to his cubicle, leaving all of us flabbergasted. While Reshu frantically dialed Jacob, who was working from home that day, to check if Sudanshu had been right, Girish offered irresistible odds to everyone around that the man would be spot on. After a brief conversation, during the course of which Reshu's eyes had grown as wide as saucers, she turned to us and confirmed that the nail polish was indeed what Sudanshu had said it was.

The same Sudanshu would fail miserably when it came to more 'manly' pursuits. On one occasion, Aman asked him, "Sud, we are all going to the Chinnaswamy this Sunday. Care to join us?"

"Is there a match on?" Sud's stock fell several points on the masculinity index with that response.

"The IPL is going on, Sud."

"Is Vivek Mallya's team playing?" It was with great effort that Aman and I restrained Girish, who had been coming to office dressed in RCB colors for the past week and who had sworn off any drink, including water, that was not a Kingfisher. Maybe Sud knew some Vivek Mallya, but he was not going to make it to the 'list of men'.

"Hey." Madhu looked and sounded super happy.

"Hi Madhu. What is the excitement all about?" I was curious

"It is still too early to say, but I absolutely must tell you, Vineet. I just filled up my internal job posting form for the team lead's position. The HR, along with Richard, spoke to me about this. They want me to apply for this position."

"Wow, Madhu! Which team is it anyway?" I happened to see Reshu's ears perking up with curiosity from behind her workstation.

"Sh...Sh...Quiet. No one really knows about it. It is the retail programming division." Madhu whispered to me.

"Retail! Madhu, what a cool break it would be for you! By the way, Reshu had kind of let me in on the news a while ago."

I watched Madhu flit away happily towards her cabin, like a carefree butterfly. What a dramatic change the girl had undergone since she had first walked into the office about two years ago! Then, she had looked disinterested in everything around her. It would come to my notice much later that she had had severe doubts on whether Bangalore was where she wanted to be. Madhu had not walked into my list of friends right away. It was only after I discovered the little girl in her, who could find happiness in the smallest of things, that we became friends. I realized that this intelligent, level-headed girl was quite capable of managing both tough projects as well as home equally efficiently.

"Vineet, meet me at the conference room." I just had time to see Sudanshu disappear into the corridor leading to the many conference rooms.

In the end, the time I took to zero down on him proved longer than the time it took to wind up the meeting. When the main agenda of the meeting is for one man to happily dump the entire project on another, it should really not take too much time, should it? It was no wonder, then, that Sudhanshu walked out with a wicked grin on his face.

"*Dai*, it is nearing one and no one is talking about lunch!" It was a good fifteen minutes to one, but then Girish liked to build up an already formidable appetite further by talking about food.

He ambled towards Aman's workstation, where I was standing, and took a good look at the printouts I was holding.

"What man? CPRI project? You are fucked. Sudanshu had briefed all of us about it, looking for volunteers to take the load off his delicate shoulders. We all shuffled our feet. No, wait, I think Tonjamba Singh, our Manipuri friend didn't shuffle his feet. That is only because his feet did not reach the floor even though he was seated. I think he stared at the ceiling, instead. Sudhanshu is lucky to have hooked you, Vineet. Now can we please go for lunch."

I was famished, myself. So when Aman showed no signs of getting off the phone with his wife, we threatened to cart him bodily over to the pantry.

Meetings upon meetings. It was another packed day.

"Asha, are we using the Zebra template?"

"No, Vineet. None of the templates were easy. We have modified the Bintus-Zed. You may want to take a look."

Admittedly, I had a tough time understanding all this template business. I often wondered if I was even cut out to be a team lead. My chain of thoughts about my ability to lead teams went like this. I thought it was all a waste of time. If that was the case, wasn't I better off wasting my time elsewhere? Perhaps, I could be a consultant at a BMW showroom, or a travel guide, or maybe even a wine tester! The last said would have been perfect. Considering that I was the last link in an unbroken line of engineers and doctors from my father's side, it would also have been the most blasphemous. A wine tester, therefore, would not only have been unique, but also that one black sheep of the family that kept gossipers like Susheela aunty in business. If mom was to be believed, I had been supplying the likes of this particular aunty enough fodder with my divorce.

While I was trying to break my head over the codes, my desk phone rang, making me nearly jump out of my skin. There was a good reason for that. The phone had not rung in the last six months. It had just sat there like some glorified paperweight. Six months ago, it had been a far more sinister device…an instrument of doom! It was the recession and people were being laid off their jobs left, right and center. And the desk phones had been the harbingers of bad news!

But, hadn't I just been made co-lead on a project? I picked the phone with a bit of uncertainty. "Vineet." I answered.

"Hi Vineet. Could you come to the HR?"

"Hello." For a fleeting second, visions of me as a wine tester in some remote lab floated across my mind.

"Mr. Vineet Hariharan. We are sorry, but we have to hand this letter over to you. Please come in."

"You idiot! Get back to work." Girish had tried this stunt once before with Aman. I cursed myself volubly for having nearly fallen for the trick.

"Hehe. *Macha*, my place today evening, what say?"

"I am not sure. I have work." I wanted to get back to work without wasting my time.

"*Dai*, please. Come over. The evening promises to be just right to get totally wasted." I could see that all the kingfishers he had downed over the IPL season had still done nothing to slake Girish's thirst. How the hell did the man get through all the work at office!

"Alright, *da*." I needed one drink today. It had been quite some time, I conceded.

I quickly started wrapping up my work for the day.

In his exuberance to have me over, Girish had forgotten that his roommate's family had landed that very evening and occupied every nook and cranny of the two bedroom flat that they shared. I was more than happy to postpone the *tanni* session to another day, but Girish would have none of it. At one time, his Facebook status read, "The basic difference between work and *tanni* is that while the former can be postponed, the latter cannot." At about half past eight, therefore, I found myself driving my Facebook philosopher and *tanni* connoisseur friend to that abandoned flat in Chandranagar. The closer I got, the more assailed I was with 'Meera thoughts' and the heavier my heart grew.

"*Macha*, I must say this. I am missing Meera. She used to be so happy whenever I came over. Though I used to mess up the place and empty her refrigerator, she was only too glad to serve me dinner." Girish was only half way through his first beer. So, he could not have been drunk. The moron actually thought Meera liked him!

"*Da*, chuck your emotions out the window. Drink up, man."

"Yeah, right. Actually, considering how both of you respected me so much, I could have done my bit to save your marriage. I should have come more often. So, there is a teeny-weeny bit of guilt in my heart." Girish slipped his arm around my shoulders in a chummy sort of way. I bottoms-upped my beer, trying desperately to steer the topic into less-controversial waters. "Did you try the new recliner?"

We watched an EPL game and a re-run of an India-Sri Lanka series through the night. I had done all I could to stock up the fridge for the night and Girish was doing all he could to empty it.

"*Macha*, do you miss, Meera?"

"I have better things to think of." It was weird that Girish should mention Meera, considering I had just been thinking about her. What a coincidence, considering I had only been thinking about her once every two minutes or so!

"*Dai*, say it. You need to release the load." Girish's face contorted and he lifted one of his sumo-wrestler butts off the floor for a second. As his face relaxed, it was clear that he had done some load releasing himself. I ran out of the room, holding my nose in disgust.

"How did Meera agree to marry you in the first place?"

I came back into the room cautiously, waving my palm to ward off any residual traces of the chemical attack. I was dying to empty the beer on that fart's head for what he had just done and also for what he had just said. But the deep respect that I had cultivated towards alcohol over the years stayed my hand.

"Look at her. She is so smart and beautiful. You were lucky, man." Girish snickered.

I emptied the beer all over his head. For good measure, I emptied a jug of water as well. All that the man said was, "Hey, man! Don't waste all that beer. If you want to pour it, pour it into my mouth."

After the beer-drenching session was done, we squatted on the floor. "You are right. She is smart and capable. She deserves someone else... not me.'

"I was kidding, Vineet. Look, all the girls in our office like you. Be it Madhu or that team lead from Sales, who has not even spoken to you. You are the handsome dude that makes the pot-bellied, nerdy, boring Software Engineers club look good, man."

"Can you explain, then, why my life sucks? I have a broken marriage. The looks are all deceptive. I just want to have a peaceful life. It doesn't work for me. My parents do not understand me. To them, I am a perfect son, to be exhibited in a showcase to the world. The whole world spoke so high of me. No wonder it all came crashing down with this divorce." I regretted having emptied all the alcohol on Girish.

"None of us have a perfect life, Vineet. See, I am the last person to advise somebody, but I seriously think that you can still have a great life." Girish sounded absolutely sober and dead serious.

"I like Meera, Girish. I am not sure why she walked away. I hate the fact that soon, just to move on, I might have to start hating her, too."

"*Macha*, let us go out for a smoke." Girish and I walked around the apartment block for some time. I had never explored the place before. To me, it had always been from the parking lot to the flat and vice-versa.

"Vineet, remember that night when you came to my house, all hassled, saying that Meera was out with her friends and was going to be late? All it took was one message from her to drive away your blues. You disappeared from my apartment faster than the beer disappears on New Year's man! You have no idea how I missed you while drinking all that beer by myself that night." Girish looked more ridiculous than he usually did, trying as he was to work up a hurt expression.

"You? Missed me?" I paused.

"Not really. Not after the first beer." He grinned.

We were now near the gate. I could see the stretch outside where Meera used to park her car. "She was out with some friends that day and had not thought it necessary to tell me. And, I, like an idiot, had planned to take her out that day. I was tired of all the fighting and wanted to do all I could to make my marriage work. I was consciously attempting to keep her happy. But then she messaged me saying that she was with her friends and would be late. I was worried for her, Girish. I always was. But she didn't ever bother to acknowledge it." While I knew that smoking made one lightheaded, I had never known how heavy it made the heart!

"Did you try talking to her about how worried you were?" Girish's voice was unusually quite.

Girish was right! I had never let Meera know how I felt for her. We had never really spent time together, during our courtship or after that. I used to worry for her, definitely, but never let her know. Come to think of it, she knew nothing about me at all. We were like strangers under the same roof.

"The day after my plan to take her out had crashed, I had wanted to take her out to lunch. She could not come because the bloody chairman of her two-bit company had to be given preference over her husband of a few months!" I looked at Girish as if he owed me an explanation for Meera's behavior.

"Come on, man. You will always get offered excuses, ranging from genuine to lame. You can either keep complaining about them and make a mountain out of a mole hill, or ignore them and go on like a superstar." Girish was gloating over the Facebook status-worthy statement he had just made. It was clearly his day.

"It is too late, Girish. You know what gift she gave me on my birthday? A grand announcement that she wanted to get separated. She walked out on me without even bothering to let me come to terms with her decision. I had just woken up and had been really looking forward to a wonderful day, when she broke the news. I vaguely remember her trying to say a lot of things, even as my body and brain struggled to wake up. I went to get some coffee for myself to recover from the bad news and the next thing I know is that she was packing her clothes!"

Girish gave me a reassuring look. "*Macha*, you cannot do much about it right? Or can you?"

"Yeah, not much I can do." I looked away from him.

"Vineet, all our lives suck man. Come on." Girish persuaded me to go another round around the building.

"Look at me *da*. I start my day promising not to overeat. But by lunchtime, my resolution breaks. I walk around with a big fat belly, fully aware that no girl in the office or anywhere else gives me a second look. Oh, actually they do but only to snigger behind my back or pass some snide remarks. You can go through five divorces, Vineet, and still have a better chance than I have of finding someone." He took the cig from my hand.

"That's not it, Girish. Look at Aman. So devoted to his wife. Look at Reshu. She is so happy. I wish that my marriage was half as good as hers. Reshu might complain about her in-laws but aren't she and Jacob perfect for each other?"

Girish took a deep drag at the cigarette. "You think so, Vineet? You don't know about this, but if it makes you feel any better, let me tell you. Jacob cheats on Reshu, *Macha*. Do you remember the time when we had gone out for lunch at the Garden Restaurant? Reshu and I were the last to leave that place and we saw Jacob with another girl. Reshu broke down in front of me and then told me all about Jacob. She had even caught him red handed once, but that seems to have made no difference to him. He coolly asked her to walk out of his life, knowing fully well that she could not. After all, hadn't her parents orphaned her because she had gotten married to a Christian?"

I stopped in my tracks. Reshu was going through such shit in her life! And I would have never guessed it the way she went on about her Jacob. Girish was so wrong. How could this make me feel better!

"She doesn't want to split with Jacob because she is clinging on to some crazy hope that he is going to mend his ways." It was shocking news and all the more difficult to believe as it was happening to a dear friend, the sweetest of the lot.

"I did not want to tell you all about this, ever. But I just thought to let you know that all our lives are fucked up." Girish shook his head once, as if trying to shake off all the pain. Then, in a jiffy, he was his old goofy self again, trying to bribe the apartment security Rangaswamy to help us pick some more beer. Rangaswamy did what he was best at. He politely refused.

"I feel bad for Reshma." We were walking back to the apartment.

For a second, the serious Girish surfaced. "Yeah man. And it is not his wife that Aman talks to everyday just before lunch." Girish walked into the apartment with a sly smile.

Somehow, the news of Aman having a casual affair did not affect me much. After freezing for a second, I shrugged my shoulders and followed Girish into the apartment. Reshma, however, had affected me deeply. That lovely girl deserved a better life any day.

The next day Girish and I walked into the office with heavy heads. We were not only late for the meeting, but were also not able to get any work started on the CPRI. Reshu walked up to me and crinkled her nose. "Hmmm.. You could have at least had a bath, Vineet."

I smiled as she walked away, happily tapping at everyone's desk. I just wished her all the happiness that she deserved.

MADHU

It had been many months since Meera and I had parted ways at Deepak's office. And I was finally ready to move on. After that momentous *tanni* session at Chandranagar, Girish and I had decided to mend our ways. That was not to say we were forsaking beer or anything. On the contrary, we decided to regularize the sessions. Our newfound respect for order was spilling over into other things in life as well. For example, as a first step towards making Girish irresistible to girls, we planned many diet charts for him. To keep his spirits up, I even volunteered to follow the diets with him, trying hard to ignore his occasional deviations from the plans, namely at breakfast, lunch and dinner every day. The outcome was that I started looking leaner and fitter, while Girish continued to accumulate the pounds.

Then I was infected by the travel bug and promptly passed it on to Girish and Aman. We decided to travel around and see the wonderful places in and around our beautiful state, to start with. We worked on a bucket list of places to visit. Soon, our circle of influence grew in radius to include places in Andhra, Tamil Nadu and my own Kerala. I bought myself a 1984 model Royal Enfield Bullet and soon we became a biker's gang of sorts. All our weekends were spent travelling. Both, Girish and I never tired of seeing new places. It helped me move on.

Madhu was inching closer to that promotion. Reshu kept

herself occupied over the weekends taking classes ranging from cookery to Spanish. Aman and his wife were on their way to having their second child. Girish and I were still single and all happy.

At home, things were beginning to settle a bit. *Ma* was busy with the temple and related activities. Papa was also visibly relaxing around me, a fact demonstrated in no small measure by the occasional conversations that he initiated. Over time, I realized how eagerly I looked forward to these little sessions with him.

"Hi Vineet!" Deepak's phone call took me by surprise.

"Hey Deepak. After so long! How have you been?" The call was a reminder that the date of the final hearing was upon me.

"Tomorrow is the eighteenth of September. Will you come over to my office? I have called Meera as well. She had not forgotten about it."

I did not think about it anymore. "I will be there, Deepak."

Meera needed no reminders. She had been long waiting for this. My case was a little different… but I was fine.

"Hey, Vineet." Sudanshu had popped up out of nowhere, even as I had just finished talking to Deepak.

"Hi, Sudanshu."

"We are celebrating the quarter-end. It has been good feedback for all of us. We are all going to Leela's. Be ready at six. We will leave together." Sudanshu was going around the floor, personally inviting everyone for the party. I wondered if I should be expecting personal letters of invitation written in flowery font on pink sheets of paper, next.

I was more than happy to party. I wanted to go out. I wanted a break from the news that Deepak had just announced. My gang got together. I was driving the girls to the place, while Aman and Girish were coming together.

The party was crazy. All the engineers wasted no time in getting stone drunk. It took only a while longer for them to shed their inhibitions, get on the dance floor and perform local acts to Shakira's and Beyonce's numbers. The *piece-de-resistance* was Basavaraj's seductive number to the tunes of "*Tonight I am loving you*". Now, Basavaraj raunchily gyrating in a tight t-shirt and a tighter pair of jeans is about the most revolting thing you'd ever get to see. However, Aman, Girish and I were thoroughly enjoying the performance from the sidelines, because the person at the receiving end of Basava's affections was none other than Sudanshu. Basava would wake up the next day and deeply regret having attempted to seduce his own boss, we knew, but there wasn't much we could do to prevent it. So might as well enjoy it. In fact, we boys had a whale of a time watching everyone make bloody fools of themselves, trying to move different parts of their bodies in sync with the music and one another. The girls were unusually quiet. Some of them were amused and some positively horrified, I thought. With eyes as big as saucers, they pointed out to the ghastly moves their male colleagues were making. While Lakshmi pointed pointedly at Vignesh's pelvic thrusts, Suma had a tough time controlling her laughter at Madhur's snake dance. Madhur was crawling all over the floor, trying to impress the new batch of girls with his flexible body, "*See I can wriggle like a worm*". It was a sight to watch!

We were really engrossed in all the fun until Aman pointed out that none of our girls were anywhere to be seen. We took turns to go look for them, but they were not on the dance floor. They were also not picking our calls. We were beginning to get just a little worried, when Madhu called me on my cell.

"Madhu, where are you guys?"

"Vineet, Reshu received a call from Jacob. I think they just had a fight. Can one of you drop her to her house? We are at the reception."

All three of us stormed out. We saw Reshu crying bitterly at the reception. We could not make out much of what she was trying to say, but we gathered that she wanted Girish to drop her home. Girish took my car, and Aman tagged along. So, the task of dropping Madhu home fell upon me. We asked Reshu to text us as soon as things turned better at home, promising to land up at her place if the message didn't come.

I kick-started Girish's bike. "We go, Madhu?

It was quite a cold night and Madhu and I had a long way to go. I was also not exactly dressed to keep the cold out.

"How is Meera?" I could barely hear Madhu, thanks to the strong wind.

"Not sure. She must be fine." I had to push up the visor a bit and shout to answer her.

"I always thought that I should have spoken to her to let her know that I wasn't having an affair with her husband." Fuck! She knew? Girish must have told her. That big mouth!

"No Madhu. It was all made up. I am sure she knows that it is not true. You cook up reasons when you have nothing else to save your ass, I think." I was very embarrassed.

"Well, I wouldn't say that she was entirely wrong." I pretended that I hadn't heard what Madhu had just said. What was that about, now? Madhu was untying her scarf.

We rode on in silence till we reached her place. I knew that the entire office had been gossiping about Madhu having a crush on me. Could it be true? I had to hear it from her. Suddenly, I wanted to go up to her apartment with her and ask her what she had meant by that comment.

"Vineet, do you want to come up for some time?"

I sat in her living room, as Madhu pottered about in her kitchen making coffee for me. Coffee after alcohol was not exactly my style, but I realized that a mug in hand would be comforting in case things turned embarrassing.

"You said something on the way, Madhu." My theory about the coffee mug being comforting went flying out the window. I was embarrassed to the core.

"Don't be so naïve, Vineet. The entire office knows about it."

"Know what?" I had to act naïve.

She gave me that stop-playing-around look. "Well, I have this huge crush on you, Vineet. I had always wanted to tell you, but I was hoping you would initiate the topic. When you told me you were marrying Meera, I spent days crying over it. Reshu was my only witness and I made her swear to keep it a secret. But then, I got over it. Meera and you were married and I was out." Madhu was not even looking at me. She was staring at some Vineet Hariharan who lived in her coffee mug.

She went on. "Honestly, I felt very bad when you guys broke up. It's tomorrow, isn't it?" She even knew about the date! Maybe all girls are good at remembering dates. Could that be why Meera had remembered the date as well? Perhaps it was not because she had been so looking forward to it as I had thought!

"Vineet, today, when I was sitting beside you in the car on the way to the Leela, I felt my feelings for you rise again. Perhaps it had always been there. Just lying dormant. I couldn't help feeling deliriously happy." Madhu was now glancing at me occasionally.

I was absolutely tongue-tied. I just managed to croak in a rather husky voice, "I always thought that the office guys were making it up. That goes for our gang as well."

Madhu looked at me. "I know that you like Meera a lot, Vineet. I knew that I would perhaps never fit in your life, but I could not stop myself from liking you."

Madhu was a special friend to me. I was not sure if we would succeed where Meera and I had failed. Somehow, compared to the highly complicated Meera, Madhu stood out as someone extremely sane.

"Madhu, you are a special girl and you should know that. You are pretty and smart and half the guys in office would give their right arm for a chance to go out with you."

"Would you want to go out with me, Vineet?" Madhu's voice was a choked whisper.

"Madhu, I always loved talking to you. Before I got married, I'd look for opportunities to spend time with you. After I got married, I just couldn't go on like that, could I? It would just give the gossipers a chance to go on about us. I was absolutely sure in my mind that you had to be protected at all times. While I was going through the worst moments of my life, I was careful not to pull you into the picture. That's the only reason I held myself back, in spite of wanting to come over and vent my heart out to you." I had not talked so much to Madhu in a long time. I could not but wonder at the irony of it all pouring out on the eve of my divorce.

Madhu held my hands. We stayed there on the couch like that for a long time, speaking occasionally, but mostly just finding comfort in each other. My phone beeped, snapping us out of our reverie. It was Reshu, informing us that things were fine at home. Though we were not sure if that was indeed the case, we realized that we had no other option than to accept it as it was. Madhu attempted to pull her hands away gently, but, suddenly, I just didn't want to let go. Instead, I pulled her to me. We were kissing each other deeply. I had a fleeting thought of how often I had imagined this. That night, we made love. Uninhibited and free of guilt. We had broken a barrier that had been nearly four years in the making. Later, as she slept peacefully, I thought how what I had fantasized had just happened between us. Was there a future to this? I made up my mind to ask Madhu out the next day.

The next morning, Madhu woke me up and pressed a cup of steaming hot coffee into my hands. The first thing that she told me was that she had gotten over me completely. She had absolutely no intention of taking this any further.

As I sipped the coffee, I stole a few furtive glances at her, wondering what had come over the girl who had admitted to having such a huge crush on me. I then realized that it had been nothing more than an infatuation for her and I had been merely living out a fantasy. I understood her completely. 'We' did not make any sense. Later, at her door, she sent me off. We did not even kiss a goodbye. We were over.

I rode to Deepak's office on Girish's bike. I thought about Madhu all the way. It was the first ever break off I had ever had, which was totally devoid of emotion.

As I parked the bike, I saw Meera standing at the entrance to the building. I walked up to her without a trace of guilt or regret for what had happened between me and Madhu. I realized that it was all in one's mind. Sometimes things happen for no apparent reason. You just let them happen.

I walked into Deepak's office. He had our file open on his desk. Without a hint of hesitation, I asked, "Where do I sign, Deepak?"

None answer'd this; but after Silence spake A Vessel of a more ungainly Make: "They sneer at me for learning all awry; What! Did the Hand then of the potter shake?"

– from the *Rubaiyat of Omar Khayyam*

Part 2 - Meera

PROLOGUE

Life had taken a big reverse. Was I proud of the role I had played in turning my life on its head? I was walking out of a life that I had not chosen in the first place. Nevertheless, it was still very much a part of my existence. Vineet was never mine. The separation was definitely the right decision.

But what was this void that I was feeling? Was life going to eventually limp back to normal? Would I be happy to go back to my old life and relish my independence? Of course, I would! I wasn't ruining someone else's life. And not mine, definitely. I could get back to doing all those things that I used to. I would also no longer have to wake up next to someone I did not care for. The feeling of not belonging to a marriage while still being very much a part of it, is way too horrible to express. And above all else was this nagging sense of guilt. Why was I feeling it? In my heart I had known that what had happened that evening was not right. I had still let things happen. Was it that? No, it was the marriage.

I wish I said no to Vineet then…. when it had all begun.

IT ALL BEGAN

It were the most blissful days of my life. At least, I thought of them as blissful. Or, at least I thought of that as my life.

Those were the days when my idea of a perfect evening was to hang out with my friends. Our own gang of three. Enough to paint the town red. Our friendship was the talk of the office. People who saw us together had no doubt that the bond had been forged in the very formative years of our lives. However, the truth was that we had known each other just a little over a year.

My life away from my friends was not much to speak of. Office fluctuated between bad and worse. Family was like a sweet and sour curry, with love and war providing their flavors in equal measure. Well, not quite equal, what with war having decidedly been the favored seasoning of late.

That evening had begun innocuously enough. My friends had agreed enthusiastically to an evening out. However, the first sign that things were not quite in order came when I suggested we go to Dido and was promptly vetoed by my gang. The look on Sri's face was one of exasperation. "Not again, Meera."

I did not give it much thought, then. Perhaps they just didn't feel like drinking that evening. There certainly wasn't anything more to it. It was all in my mind. It was still as perfect an evening as any, I thought, as I sat down with the two of them at Coffee Club. A little gossip would just make up for the lack of alcohol.

Was I really hearing the conversation right or does coffee make one delusional?

Husbands, children, maids, washing powder…Really? What the hell were they talking about? Were my friends wandering down the same path that Nikki had strayed on soon after marriage? I shuddered involuntarily when I remembered the conversation between Nikki and *amma* that I had inadvertently butted into that evening so many evenings ago. The topic of debate was what was the best washing powder to use to keep Amit's seven thousand rupee white shirt, sparkling white. Seeing me hanging about within earshot, *amma* had tried to rope me into the conversation. But, my question ensured that my participation was short lived. "Nikki, seven thousand rupees! Why does Amit need so many white shirts?"

I snapped back to the present. The conversation had now progressed to the price of onions. For the first time I felt out of place with my friends.

We had always had the best of times together. We could not wait to finish work to meet. I had lost count of the reasons we had cooked up to supply our boss with and get out early from work. What had happened to my cool friends? They had not wanted to go to Dido!

"Let us go to Coffee Club. Plain and simple coffee! I do not want to drink." Sridevi Vallabhan, I thought, was one of the most talented girls I had met. I also thought that the girl had just sacrificed all her talent and energy at the altar of marital bliss. And she had sounded so married when she put down my suggestion to go to Dido. From the few stray words I heard of the conversation, I gathered that she was already planning to have babies. Apparently, her biological clock (I wonder which unimaginative moron named it) was ticking away to glory at rocket speed. Well, I guess it was only in the natural course of things for her to have upgraded her boyfriend to fiancé first and then to husband. However, what was unimaginable was her utter devotion to this latest upgrade! I had once thought that I belonged to a rather elite group of people in her life. Now I was beginning to have second thoughts.

Sri had met us that day to discuss household chores! And the discussion was happening over a coffee! The combo was beginning to stress me out. How I wished I could have rolled the clock back an hour and called off the plan! I kept glancing at the door wondering if it would be rude to just bolt out of the place. Deeply engrossed as they were in some domestic discussion, they would perhaps not even notice if I left. They didn't seem to be enjoying their coffee or anything. Why on earth had they not let me have some alcohol then? They could have gossiped in Dido as well, couldn't they?

"Save your system from alcohol, Meera. De-toxification is the first step towards having a healthy baby." Charu seemed to have read my thoughts. "Hey Sri, do you want to have a boy or a girl?" Charulatha Das was my dearest friend. With almost five years of experience in the field, she was the veteran of the group and the self-certified expert on marital matters. She lived like a slave to her husband. Needless to say, our ideologies did not match, but we had discovered some deep tie that had bonded us to one another. I had felt very close to Charu right from the day we had first met. Soon, I became her closest confidante and guide on the cumbersome road called life.

Charu and Sri had been my partners in crime. Together, we had raided all food joints and bars worthy of note around town. Meet, eat, drink, gossip, stay over, sleep over, movies, fun, laughter, tears, secrets and more. There was absolutely nothing that we had not discussed or tried doing together.

Who were these people who were haggling like housewives over cups of coffee? Where were my friends?

Charu, how could you change like this? I can understand Sri sounding old, but not you darling! I sat staring at Charu, wondering if I should let her know what I had just been thinking.

"A baby girl, Charu! An angel and she has to look just like me. Not like Deepak or his family." For once, I had to agree. No child deserved to look like Deepak or any other member of his family. Hello! What were these idiots getting so excited about? The event that they were yapping about would take at least a year to happen. When had this sort of change taken place? That was the day I realized that all good things had to come to an end. My soul sisters were just like any other girls. I was the odd one there.

Sri, I really hope this is just the newly wedded effect and it wears off real quick.

After settling the bill, I could not wait to run away. I was happy to ride off. But then, the prospect of going back home was not exactly enticing either. Mom and Dad were upset with me. We hardly spoke any more. The only time *amma* spoke to me these days was to dispense advice, which made the harrowing discussion I had just endured at Coffee Club seem as thrilling as a rock concert!

I missed Steve. He was the only person I could talk to. Should I message him? Maybe not. I could handle this. I didn't need to disturb Steve. He needed to spend time with his friends. And moreover, he was not my boyfriend. I was definitely not going to message him.

I pulled my phone out of the bag, wondering if the damn thing was a blessing or a curse!

As if on cue, the phone rang. "Hi, *amma*" Mom unerringly called me at the wrong time always. "I'll be home in another twenty minutes."

"That means an hour at least! I hope you have started from the place where you were. And Meera, I do not want you going out with any of your friends anymore. You have to start coming home early. Why do you need to go out every day? Don't give me that excuse about you needing a break and all. You spend all that you earn without a care! I wonder where it goes. Your father or I don't get any of it. All you do is to spend it on your jobless friends." Mom invariably ended up calling my friends 'jobless' or other variants of that adjective and it invariably made me see red.

"Mom! You and dad do not need my money. Dad is earning well. He does not need my meager salary. And I do not understand the need to talk about it now." It wasn't entirely mom's fault. The disappointment of an evening ill-spent was beginning to boil over and rage into a fight. I could have picked up a fight with anyone unfortunate enough to have crossed my path then.

"Meera, is that the way to talk to your mother? We don't need your money. We have saved enough to support ourselves. But what do you have to rely upon? All this money that you spend without a care can add up to a fortune." Mom and her unending drama had begun.

"I spend about two hundred rupees at the coffee shop...or five hundred at the most. How is that going to add to a fortune, *amma*?" I knew that the argument was simply a waste of time. Mom was not going to buy that, ever.

"This is the trouble with you and your sister. Both of you do not know the value of money. You need to save all the small two hundreds to make that fortune. And..."

"*Amma*, cops around. I have to hang up. Bye *ma*, I will see you." I hung up on her while I could still hear her speak. I was simply not in the mood to listen, right then.

Mum and dad were upset with me. In fact, I had been fighting with everyone. Work life was bad. Love life was worse (for the simple reason that there was no love in my life). Friends were busy setting up their own homes and hearths. And I needed a break. I badly needed one!

I played some music on my phone. It would not help me avoid calls, but it would definitely bring back the 'me' time. The slight breeze and minimal traffic acted like a stress buster. Hmm...

peace. I was thinking about Steve.

Why was Steve not my boyfriend yet? Should I ask him? If Sri was to be believed, I looked desperate when he was around. So I should just ask him. *No, Meera, it is bad enough to look desperate. You don't want to start sounding that way, as well.* Aren't guys supposed to make the first move? He is so cute! Why was he away in Goa? I hoped that he was thinking about me too. Did I love him? I should be taking this slow. I need to have a boyfriend first. I did not have one in nearly two years now. And I had not had a steady boyfriend ever. Steve was perfect. I didn't have to be married to him. I am sure he didn't want it too. Could I be just his pastime?

After reaching home and having the customary brief confrontation with *amma* and *acha*, I retired to my room. Lying on my bed, I hoped that the day had been just one of those occasional bad ones and that my friends would make a grand comeback. I also hoped that Steve would be back in town soon.

AT WORK

"*Guys, a great effort! We have a reason to celebrate. All of us have met our targets. I would like to congratulate each one of you. Keep up the good work and... your efforts to continue.*" Anil Bakshi was our Regional Head and the biggest turn off within the radius of fifty miles. He was the perfect manager that no organization could do without. He honestly believed that management was all about delivering utterly uninspiring pep talks. What he'd never understand was that students of the fourth grade delivered more meaningful speeches. He was tailor-made for sales and universally voted as the 'most hated' manager by all employees. If I had to describe him in one word, I would, for the lack of a better word, describe him as 'CHEAP'. The 'better' words would be too colorful to print.

The office cheered and applauded the numbers they had achieved. I too had a number that I had not achieved in a very long time. It was a number that was determined by some guy who sat in some remote corner of the world and had absolutely no clue about me or the market I had to deal with. I knew that Mr. Cheap would call for me the moment he retired to his cabin, to grill me on my 'failure'. The guy had directed looks loaded with meaning my way all through the speech he made. God, what was in store for me!

"Meera! Bakshi wants to see you in his cabin. I had warned

you about it, hadn't I? Just because the team met with the overall targets, things are not going to be fine for all us. He is going to ask us about the large deals that we missed this quarter. Only you did not meet the target, Meera. The team covered it up for you. Just keep your calm and meet me at the cafeteria after the meeting." Sanjay was my team leader and best colleague to whom I could vent out my frustration at any time of the day. He had always been an inspiration to me even in the most testing of times. I wondered how a man could smile through his problems as well as his team's. He covered up for me most times in front of Bakshi, by letting him know that the missed targets were to do with the absurd numbers, rather than my lack of ability. In fact, he had gone out of his way many times to invent illnesses to explain my absence from office, while I was out relishing 'Chocolate Fantasies' at coffee outlets near the office. And most importantly, he was someone that I could relate to in the office filled with jerks.

"Alright Mr. Bakshi, let us meet!" I pulled myself up with great reluctance.

"Hi, Anil!" I entered his cabin to be greeted by the sight of a poor keyboard being thumped mercilessly by sausage-sized fingers. I wondered what the man did the entire day! Susan composed his mails. She organized his meetings, canceled them and passed the message on his behalf. If given his role, she was sure to perform better. But the world was not exactly fair to the many Susans' and Meeras' that inhabited it.

"Come in." He did not even lift up his head to look at me.

I sat on the edge of the rather oversized chair. While he continued hammering that keyboard, my eyes wandered across the room and fell on a shiny bit of glass on the floor. It looked vaguely familiar. I was sure that he would soon stop the pounding and bring up the $50K deal that had been due for a long time now. And, I thought I had an answer.

Sure enough, he gave one last key-dislocating tap to the

keyboard and turned to me with a gap-toothed smile. "So, Meera...Meera...Good day it is. But not great for you and me!". Aargh! His plastic smile irritated me.

"This is the eighth quarter in a row that you have missed your targets. Tell me! How can I help you? Your login times are bad. Your acquisition targets are not great. Is it the approach that you are faltering on? Or, don't get me wrong, but are there personal issues? You can tell me. You know I am a good guy."

I wished! And I wanted to pass the question. But...

"Anil, I can defend myself here. I had been performing for three years until you chose to give me a set of accounts that have refused to transact with Nexter for the almost five to seven years now. I am trying my best to convert some of the dead accounts with a few small deals to start with. And I believe it is a very good start for me, you and Nexter. I have the count as well, Anil. It is seventeen accounts that have restarted doing business with us. I do not need a trainer to help me sell. I just need a couple of large accounts that can help me earn money.

My personal issue is that I have neither been able to earn incentives in the last two years nor have been even remotely considered for a promotion. I have stayed stuck to the same role in the same place and watched people grow and move past." I proudly sat back in the chair, confident that my words were going to shut him up for good on the subject. After all, my point was valid and any human being would be able to understand it. This is where I had overestimated my boss!

"Meera, there are two things that I would like to let you know." This was another classic Anil Bakshi trait. He always had 'two things' to tell everyone.

"Firstly, you are our star performer. You cannot settle for easy accounts. Show to the world that you are the best. You have it in you, Meera." Bakshi was on his second pep talk of the day!

"Secondly, being a very good employee does not help. You

need to be smart and hardworking Your call rates are very low. You have been very irregular to work. How are you going to build a relationship with customers?"

"Thirdly, …"

I knew that this was coming! If Anil Bakshi said there were two things he had to tell someone, that someone could rest assured that there were at least three things, if not more. How did the moron even clear his third grade if he could not keep count! Damn! There were three things he had to complain about? Or maybe more?

"Thirdly, you have not been attending any of the trainings or product meetings. How will you learn about the new updates?" He leaned back on his chair and started to rock it. The smug look that had been cavorting on my face a minute ago was now resting comfortably on his face.

I could have said quite a few things to wrest that look back from his face, but I restrained myself.

"Alright Anil, I will try my best to achieve my targets this quarter."

"That's the spirit, Meera! I want you to attend the personality development training tomorrow. Ok, now get back to work." With that, the man got back to pounding the poor machine.

I left Bakshi's cabin and made straight for the cafeteria. "Sanjay, please pass me the smoke. Light another one for yourself." The first puff brought with it a sense of relief, but I needed something stronger than tobacco to clear my head.

"Hey, how was your meeting? Did Bakshi behave well?" Sanjay looked as calm as ever. I could never understand that expression of his. He was in as much trouble as I was. But, he had always kept his cool, something that I found quite impossible to match.

"Bad, worse and ugly. Like always, none of my problems were solved. Well, I wasn't expecting them to be, either. So, I decided to agree to whatever he asked for. He was complaining about me being irregular. I am not sure as to when that happened. He wants me to attend the same drab product trainings that have not changed even by a comma since thier inception. I have been selling stuff for five years now. He should trust my knowledge on these products. But, he would not understand."

I took another drag at the cigarette. "Oh, by the way, he broke the crystal that we gave him on his birthday." My brain had finally managed to identify the shiny bit of glass that I had seen in Bakshi's cabin as a part of that expensive gift we had given that worthless piece of trash a month ago. Phew! Curious case solved.

"Did he not ask you about that famous deal of yours, Meera?"

"Well," I said, blowing a thin stream of smoke, "I am glad that he didn't."

"Did he say anything about your promotion?"

"Was he supposed to? Is there something? Oh! Please say yes, Sanjay."

"No I do not know. I was thinking that I should take it up with Anil. But I don't have the numbers to back up your case, Meera." Sanjay stubbed out his cigarette, clearly preparing to leave. He had this annoying habit of leaving conversations midway. Especially when something worthwhile was being discussed.

He had done exactly that when the subject of my promotion had come up almost a year earlier. "Come on Anil, Meera knows her work and she always steps in when one is no around. She has been with Nexter for four years and…," Sanjay had left the conversation at that point to answer his phone. And Bakshi had seized the opportunity to tell me 'two things' about why I did not deserve the promotion.

"There is no excuse this quarter. I understand that the targets have always been high. But, my dear, that to you is sales. This quarter you have a small breather. Your targets are reasonable. So you got to perform. Now, let us go back to work." Sanjay walked towards the lift, seemingly not caring if I was keeping pace. He indicated that I should stub out the barely-lit cigarette in my hand. My heart always breaks when I have to do that. Sanjay never smoked his cigarette fully. The one thing I cannot stand is a smoker not valuing a cigarette!

The lift door opened to our floor. Suddenly, a wave of nausea hit me. I just hated the thought of going back to my cubicle. The ambience was so claustrophobic! Reminded me of my classroom back in school. Yeah…it was every bit like those classrooms. The boring teachers were replaced with even more boring bosses. That was the only difference!

A smoke break never failed to instill a sense of enlightenment in me. In its nirvana-like state, my mind revealed to me the ultimate truths of the corporate world, such as "*The smoking zone is the ideal place to work in an organization*" or "*Nicotine amplifies Productivity.*" Alcohol also never failed to invoke the philosopher within me. Two beers down and I would attain the attitude of a guru and pass down pearls of wisdom to my ardent devotees, Charu and Sri. "When I start a company of my own, employees will be entitled to free beer and humor. I will show to the world that in beer there is productivity and in water there is bacteria."

"Hey Meera." I had been spot on with my analysis. Sri was definitely sounding so married! Maybe it was time to move her to my list of uncool friends.

"Hiii. How goes it?" I asked.

"Work is fine. By the way, my sister-in-law delivered a baby boy this morning. I sent you a message. Did you get it? Aww! He is soooo cute." Sri went on and on in spite of the fact that I had switched her off somewhere between the 'hey' and the 'baby boy'.

What on earth was happening around me? I despised work. I was just planning to hang around till I got a chance to prove my worth. Or, till I got that promotion that was long due.

Of the phone on my desk rang and for once I was thankful. That was the only way Sri would have stopped yapping about her new family and their exploits. Seriously, was having a baby really all that difficult? My sister had had two without too much trouble and here was Sri who was making it sound like some war plan that had to be thoroughly analyzed, dissected and signed in triplicate before being put into action. She had been venturing into how she planned to handle this phase of her life with a calendar and folic acids and various pills for good measure, when I was literally saved by the bell.

I answered the phone.

"Hello sir, good morning."

"Yes, I will send you the details."

"I am sorry but not before the 23rd."

"The custom clearance part will take time."

"I will do my best. I will have the delivery expedited. But I am sorry I cannot promise you, sir. I am really sorry about that."

"Yes, the software kit is added, and for free. It will not show up in your invoice copy. But it is definitely added."

"Thank you, sir. Have a great day."

"Should we expedite any order, Meera?" Bhaskar was my dear man in the logistics team. Interacting with the logistics team had always been a challenge for me. And my short temper had not helped matters. Bhaskar was one among the two men in my life who loved me unconditionally. The other man was Daddy. Or so I liked to tell myself.

"No Bhaskar, The call was from Neon Consulting. The guy who demands a 'quick turnaround time', even if his orders are outlandish! We should just ignore him. I will handle this. Thanks for asking." I smiled very flirtatiously at Bhaskar, who walked away stealing occasional shy glances at me.

The rest of the day was very mundane. No new customers, processing some of the old orders, a few calls here and there, a boring lunch and a few more smoke breaks. I wanted to go out but since Charu and Sri were not even remotely interested, I had to head home.

If I had been driving a car, I could have smoked all the way.

VEEDU... MY HOME

"Meera, what happened, dear? Are you alright?"

"I am, *amma*? Why, what happened?" I was worried.

"It is barely six and you are already home!" *Amma* was laughing at me.

Ah! Sarcasm. That which mom had raised to an art level! For a fleeting second I wondered if something had been smeared on my face!

"I am so happy to see you home early. Looks like Charulatha and Sridevi have finally abandoned you for their husbands. And that's exactly how things have to be, Meera. After marriage a girl has to lead a responsible life. How long will you wander around aimlessly? It will be wise to get married at this age. You will be left all alone otherwise. Parents always have the best interests of their children in mind. Stay positive! If you agree, we can arrange for you to meet a few boys. Also, please do not have a lot of expectations. Look at your sister! Well, initially we did oppose her affair with your brother-in-law. But now, we are very happy for her. How well she takes care of Amit and the children! You have a lot to learn from her." *Amma* had delivered this momentous speech in the time it took me to walk from the door to the couch in the living room.

I could have spared *amma* the effort of having rendered that particular speech. Having heard it about a zillion times, I could repeat it word-for-word. Why did mom and even dad to an extent, have to indulge in these 'character comparisons' between their offspring? The fact that Nikki was the ideal daughter that they could have ever hoped for, was well established. In addition, she was also the best wife that Amit, the traveling businessman, could ever hope to find. To top it all, she had also proved to be the best mom to Manu and Paru, ensuring that her kids got the best of everything, right from education, to clothes, to multiple classes. The kids, aged five and three, were so busy that they had already been programmed to take power naps! I had once tried to gently persuade Nikki to go easy on the kids and introduce them to the games of the eighties and the nineties, only to be soundly rebuked with a curt, "I want my kids to stay ahead in the race. When you have one, we will have the child brought up on I-spy and land or water." Were these games that bad, I had wondered. After all, both Nikki and I had been brought up on a steady diet of games like these and not turned out so badly.

"*Amma*! Would you please stop? I am in no state of mind to go through this again. Please *amma*." I could not look or behave like Nikki *chechi*. But, she was the benchmark. I would need a tremendous makeover even to think of meeting that yardstick of perfection. Maybe, Bakshi's personality development training was what I needed!

"Ok! Let me not say anything. You do whatever you feel like. But as a mother, I am worried for you. You are growing old. Is it my fault? What do I do? I have hundreds of people to answer to." *Amma's* voice had already begun to choke.

"*Amma*, when I am ready to get married, I shall find someone myself." There. I couldn't have stated it better! The conversation had to end absolutely. Given the amazing rapport I shared with my mom, I simply couldn't let the topic drag.

"So, you are going to find a boy on your own? Oh! So you will follow in Nikita's steps." I wished she'd make up her mind about this. Was I or was I not supposed to follow Nikki's example?

She continued. "You know that we did not want her to get married to Amit, right! But she was adamant. It is just that things worked out well for her. Nikki is a mature girl and knows very well how to manage things. Even assuming that you are capable of handling your life, things are not easy for you. *Acha* will not accept anyone who does not belong to our community into the family again."

Community, that invisible, omnipresent, omnipotent monster had raised his ugly head and given Meera a vicious bite again!

"Community? Who is this community *amma*? Latha *maami*? Gokul *mama*? Who gives them the right to interfere with our lives? They say whatever comes to their mind about your own daughter…nothing flattering, I am sure…and you still call them your own community!"

"Meera! Do not talk about your elders like that." *amma* snapped. "Whatever they say is for your own good. If you think that you can get away with this indifferent attitude of yours, go ahead. I will not interfere in your affairs, ever. But mark my words, Meera. This attitude of yours will take you nowhere. One day you will realize how wrong you were."

Of late mom had been sounding increasingly like a religious preacher of sorts, I attributed this to the influence of some holy godwoman she had been visiting. It had started two months ago, if my memory serves me right. She had come home one evening, looking very pious and a little bit distressed at the same time. Apparently, this godwoman had convinced mom that she had been sent to earth by God himself. I had, of course, burst out laughing, leaving *amma* furious. How, she had wanted to know, could I demean someone who had just revealed to her the very meaning of life. How, she asked, could I laugh at a person who had just made her realize that money is the root of all evil. I learned later that this very root cause of all evil, a good thousand rupees worth of it, had been required to gain entry into the ashram. I then proposed to introduce *amma* and her friends to an altogether cooler meaning of life for free. *Amma* had balked visibly at the proposal.

As a consequence of my alleged disrespect towards this godly figure, an entire battalion of *amma*'s friends had landed up at our house the next day. This 'swamy army' was led by a seasoned veteran, a formidable woman to look at. That is, until you spotted her footwear. The minute I laid my eyes on this particular article of personal apparel, I lost all the awe I had accumulated for the woman. She was wearing the same pair of crocs that my little Paru wore, only several sizes bigger. This woman explained to me in what she must have hoped was a saintly voice, "Meera, it is because of your karma that you are nowhere close to discovering your inner self. Stay pure and let good thoughts flow in." After they left, I asked *amma* what exactly the woman had been trying to say. By the time *amma* had finished her explanation, my elusive inner self had packed its bags and taken the next available flight to an undisclosed location.

Back in the present…and I was just not ready to listen to what *amma* had to say. I wanted to lock myself in my room. Anger, sadness, frustration and depression colored my mood in equal measure. I took a good long look at myself in the mirror. Things were not working well in the office. Home was fast turning painful. My friends had turned into something unacceptable. I was alone…all alone. As I stood there watching myself, self-pity loomed large over me. Overcome with emotion, I was just beginning to struggle with this inner turmoil, when another more urgent inner voice called to me. Was this the voice of the inner self that the croc-wearing aunty was talking about? No. actually it was the sound of my stomach rumbling with hunger.

After having made a great show of storming into my room, I needed a strong reason to step out. I could go out on the pretext of getting my cell phone. Mmm..what was that smell!

Mum's culinary skills were at their best when we had had a fight. I contemplated the entire situation again and arrived at an unbiased conclusion that onion *pakodas* had done me no harm and deserved all respect. I went into the kitchen quickly and collected a few, pretending not to look at *amma*. Then, mustering what was left of my dignity, I ran back to the relative safety of my room.

I looked at the phone. There were three missed calls. It was Steve. Oh my God!

And there was a message – "*Hey! I reached a while ago. Are you at office? How is work?*

Having had three missed calls and a message from Steve, I conceded that it was okay to call him now.

Steve had finally called! "Hi Steve!" I was thrilled and very happy that he answered my call.

"Hi Meera! How are you?" He seemed happy to talk to me, too. "I was thinking if we could meet today".

"I would love to but got done with work early and reached home a while ago. How you been? How was Goa?" I asked.

"Oh! It was heaven. We boys had super fun. No work, no girlfriends to worry about. We kept drinking all night." Steve said.

"That sounds like fun."

"Ok, so can we meet tomorrow?" he asked.

"Sure." I replied. "We meet after work? I will see you at seven-ish. Are we good?"

"Yes Ma'am."

The meeting was fixed. But 'Yes Ma'am?' Didn't that sound sarcastic? That teasing tone of his was very evident. Well my 'Are we good' had sounded no better. I desperately needed to get rid of those Anil Bakshi slangs.

Anyways all was well. Something good was finally happening. I could not wait to meet Steve the next day. Where were we meeting? I had not asked him about that. I couldn't call him back on that. And, this time I had to make it a point to reach on time.

The rest of the evening went just fine. I spoke to Nikki. More importantly, I spoke to Manu, who was progressing through stages of imperfect grammar. It brought a smile to my face. I could hear Paru attempting to match up to her brother's language skills in her own endearing way. That was another stress buster for the evening. *Amma* and I had buried that hatchet and called a truce for the day. *Acha* was home as well. I hardly spoke to him. But it was as pleasing as ever to see him back home. It was a good night.

STEVE

For as long as I could remember, I had dreaded getting dressed for office every morning. I had a stuffed closet, yet I would cycle the same few outfits every week. But that morning was different. I had a special set to wear…a set that I had been saving for a very long time…for a very special day! The grey top and the light blue pair of jeans were not exactly remarkable by themselves, but the *piece-de-resistance* was a pair of red suede shoes. *Amma* had raised her eyebrows when she had seen my shoes for the first time, admonishing me for having spent a 'fortune' on them. According to her, the money would have been better spent in buying jewellery, which would hold its own even if my own stocks went down. My mom said the most encouraging words!

I knew that Steve was not going to notice any of it, but today was special.

I had a typical 'Bakshi day' at work – uninspiring, obnoxious and mind numbing. The man himself made his usual rounds to check if we were making calls to customers and see if any of us were on social networking and other 'non-profit-bearing' sites. But, his annoying presence made no difference to me. Charu and Sri were sounding a little better. Although Sri's husband's boss's brother's daughter's school day figured prominently in the lunchtime discussions, I was in no mood to complain.

I did not realize how happy the thought of meeting Steve had made me that day.

After three, time seemed to have ground to a halt! I was not going to call any more customers for the day. I did not want the 'happy' day to be ruined by a customer who could not understand that while the orders could wait, heavenly moments, such as the ones I hoped would be lying in store for me later that evening, couldn't. Sanjay looked curious, as he watched me across the cubicle. I could only smile back.

"Meera, what happened?" Charu was as curious as Sanjay.

"Tell me Charu," I asked eagerly, "Am I smiling at nothing? Sanjay just gave me a strange stare."

"Yeah! It is very obvious that something is cooking. Wait a minute! Are you going to meet Steve? Is he in town?" Charu asked.

I sheepishly smiled back at Sanjay and then at Charu. "Yes Charu! He is finally in town. I thought that he was never going to get bored with his boyfriends. But he called. Can you believe it!"

"What is with the red shoes? I must say that you are looking hot." I could not believe my own ears. Charu was actually saying that! She had never liked Steve, mainly for his obvious 'non-Indian-ness'. Steve is of mixed blood. He has an English mother and an Indian father, a businessman from Delhi. His parents separated when he was just a boy and his mother moved back to England, leaving Steve with his father. Steve looked Indian, but his frequent visits to England had left a profound western influence. He talked and behaved like an Englishman. That, probably, was one of the reasons why I was attracted to Steve.

"Thank you Charu. You know what? I may sound desperate, but I really hope that I get to kiss him today, Charuuuu…"

"Mad Meera! You are impossible. Now, get back to work." With that, Charu shifted her focus back to work.

I was glad that Charu did not react too badly at all. Her philosophy of love does not allow for irrational actions such as kissing or making-out with someone who is not your boyfriend (even if the opportunity presents itself on a platter.)

Six arrived. Finally! I kept glancing at my phone, wanting it to display 'Steve'. Sri and Charu were going to the canteen and I tagged along. There was no way I was going to hang around in that boring cubicle. The canteen wore a deserted look. Were people really working that hard or had they already left for the day! Well, how did it matter to me? Didn't I have better things to worry about? Like…Ah! My bag. I noticed that my bag and shoes were perfectly coordinated…the same shade of red…a deep shade that was designed to entice prospective boyfriends or so I wanted to believe. Hmmm…even unplanned things were working well for today. Sri observed that I had not smoked the entire day. I was glad about it. We were just beginning to sit down, when my prayers were answered.

I let the ringtone play out almost to the very end before answering. Didn't want to show any signs of desperation. "Hey Steve." My tone was also just right.

"Hi Meera! Shall we meet at seven? At Dido?"

"Alrightie! See you". I could not wait to leave.

"Alright darlings, I have to go. Dido is a good thirty minutes away on my bike. So, I'd better start now." I packed my bag quickly.

Sri and Charu were busy munching fries. I wondered why calorie talks never cropped up during lunch. That should put these much-married people in their place!

"Have fun! Say a big hi to Steve from us." They were still munching away those potato crisps.

I started my bike. *I should get there before Steve does. Need to set my hair and smell good. Where do I leave my helmet? Damn! The under seat storage space is full of smelly clothes. I wish I hadn't smoked so much. I could have saved place for the helmet. I am not going to walk around with that. I will leave it with the bartender and so I will have to go inside without Steve.*

At the signal, I counted every second. Then my phone beeped. It was a message from Steve. "*Heyyy, I left from office. Will see you in 20. Can't wait ☺.*"

I was grinning widely.

I first met Steve at Charu's place, almost a year ago. Charu's husband, Ansh was celebrating his promotion at home. Steve D'Sa had come to the party with some friends of his. He looked as bored as I was. Sri was dancing with Deepak, then her fiancée. Charu was so busy that she could not even spare me a look. I was on my own.

Steve looked so out of place that it was clear that parties and social gatherings were not exactly his cup of tea.

I was smoking in the balcony when Steve first approached me. "Hi. Can I borrow a light?" Steve looked very pale then, but his brown shirt was what I fell for. So I had a substantial reason to pass the light. I loved the color of his eyes. That is one of the biggest advantages of having a *firang* mother. Sometimes I wished that I were the result of an illicit liaison between Madhav K.S and some *firang*. Of course I'd never settle for anyone other than the weird but lovely Geetha Madhav for my other parent. So I was a little unclear as to how exactly I wanted the DNA mixing to have worked out. But, all I wanted was that same grey shade.

"So you are from Ansh's office." Though Steve was clearly a shy boy, he had initiated a conversation. Not bad. Someone looked interested!

"No, from Charu's…you know, Ansh's wife." I said.

"Okay, I don't know them all that well. I am here with a friend who is from Ansh's office. I am Steve." He extended his right hand, switching the cigarette to his left. I noticed that his cigarette looked more burnt on one side than lit. Was he trying his hands at smoking just to approach a girl? How endearing!

"Hi, I am Meera."

Before I knew it, I was talking to Steve about his work, his Finnish hound and even his girlfriends. There had been two of them and I realized that both had taken complete advantage of him. Alright! So he was single.

Charu sprang up from nowhere. She pulled both of us in for a dance. I danced with everyone except Deepak, whose fiancée was guarding him fiercely like a mother hen and keeping him away from all girls, including myself. Ansh is a fine dancer and we jived for a really long time.

Steve introduced me to his friends. We were just beginning to dance, when Charu decided to change the music and play romantic numbers. The combined effect of the drinks and the music was a little too much for Steve and me. I disappeared into the kitchen to grab something to eat. So hungry was I that I polished off a veg roll in three ravenous bites!

I would have to stay at Charu's. I wasn't exactly looking forward to sharing a room with a couple who would, in all probability, be making out the entire night! It was then that Steve came to my rescue. He decided to stay back with me. The apartment was within a layout, and we could easily stay outdoors without being bothered.

"Tell me something about yourself." Steve asked. We had perched ourselves on a wall that ran around the compound.

"Well, I have been working as a sales consultant in a company called Nexter for about five years now. It pays me well...so I am staying put. My family is in Bangalore with me. I have a few friends from college and work, who are close to me. I am trying hard to find ways of getting a scholarship to do my masters in the U.S. Don't ask me any more about it...I am still trying to figure it all out." I said.

"Haha, Okay. I will not ask you. But do you want to do an MBA?" Steve asked.

"Yeah, that is my plan. My experience in sales will help."

"Good and what else about you?" Steve was not interested in my boring plans. That was perfectly fine by me.

"What else? Nothing at all." I looked back at him.

"So, do you have a boy friend?" That was quick, I thought.

I wish I had not been so drunk. I obviously had a dazed pair of eyes when I told him, "No, no one." Did that make a difference to him? I was curious to know.

We were talking, laughing and smoking away. To be more accurate, I was smoking away, while poor Steve was only trying. We went up to the apartment to get some food. I had a great time talking to him. Then Steve decided to drive out to get more cigarettes. We drove quite a distance, ignoring all the petty shops close to the layout that were open even at that hour.

The security guards at the layout were not too thrilled to open the gates for us, that late. The party was long over. We would have to get out of the car and walk to the apartment. I was struggling to open the door, taking care not to bang it against a pole that was inconveniently close to it. Suddenly, Steve pulled me by my hand. "Meera…" he kissed me. He was grabbing my hand and pulling me towards him when I pulled out of the car. Something was not right. The alcohol and tobacco cushioning effect had vanished. I could not look at him. "Bye Steve".

I ran to Charu's apartment and collapsed on the sofa. In the morning, I checked to see if Steve was still around. He was not.

Life was back to being the same. Work was as mundane as ever. Home was no good, either.

A week after the party, Steve showed up at my office. He had come to apologize. I had been missing him and started liking him as well. I could not help but smile back. Steve and I became very good friends. We met every day. His friends were now my friends, too. Then, one day…

"Steve, can I ask you something?"

"Sure, honey." Steve held my hand.

"Why is it that you still haven't asked me?" I said.

"Do I need to ask?" His eyes had that dazed look, now.

I leaned to kiss him. Our first 'approved' kiss. It felt deep. And, it was a very special one.

"Is it alright now?" He was holding me close to him.

"I did not understand, Steve." I said, pulling back slightly.

"Well, it is universally alright if a girl wants to kiss. But it is not the same when we boys want to do it." Steve was smiling, but the smile had been wiped off my face.

"What was that, Steve? Are you talking about what happened that night at the party? Well, you should have known that I was not open to the idea of kissing on the first day...when I hardly knew you." The conversation was spiraling towards a fight.

"We knew each other quite well by then, Meera." Steve was still sounding calm.

"Yes, but not well enough for a kiss." I began to pack my things.

Steve was attempting to get off the fight, but I was not helping him on that.

"You know what, you should look at yourself in the mirror." He was smiling. Smiling enough to ignore the argument.

Wasn't that rude?

"I will, after we are done with this conversation." I said.

"Meera, my intention was not to blame you." Steve followed me to the door.

"Oh yeah? But you know what, Steve? Your intentions are not working all that well."

"Why do we have to fight?" I hated to see him so composed.

"I am not fighting. You made a flimsy statement which is a good enough reason to fight." I was fuming.

"Alright, Meera. I do not want to talk about this again. It was always on my mind and therefore I brought it up. I felt horrible when you walked out of the car that day. It made me feel like I was someone sleazy. I have not forced anyone. That day we spoke about so many things and I just felt like kissing someone who was laughing with me and letting me hold her hand." Steve tried to stop me.

"Yeah, it is my mistake. I should not have crossed my limits. I thought that you were not the kind of boy that takes advantage of a girl, just because she behaved nicely with you. But you know what..? I am leaving." I was not great at handling heated conversations. I choose to move away from it all, and that is exactly what I did.

Frustrated and angry, I had an unusually severe case of road rage that day. Steve was the sole reason for it.

Before long, however, I started missing him. I thought of how I had stormed out of his place, even as he was trying to stop me. Steve had been so surprised by the way I had reacted. In a calmer moment, later, even I was surprised. I wanted to go back to him the next day, but my king-sized ego prevented me from doing so.

The week following the fight was pure, unadulterated hell. I kept checking his messages. I lost count of the number of times I 'almost' called or messaged him. Every time, the same old ego would step in and force me to hit the 'back' button. Weeks progressed into months and Steve was not heard from or seen.

Then came a day when I turned twenty-six. It was not like I had an option in that matter or something, really. And god knows I have hated birthdays since I turned twenty. But it wasn't so bad. My friends, mom, dad, Nikki, Manu, Paru, and Amit made it very special for me. I had a perfect birthday. The cake was big and so were the gifts. Nikki made it extra special by picking up that top I had so wanted, but had kept away from it because of its price.

And finally, when the day was drawing to a close, Steve decided to show up in the form of a message.

He was going to Goa and wanted to see me after he returned. I replied with a 'yes'...a delayed 'yes', thanks to the 'bad' me'.

It had been seven days since that message that day. I could not wait to see him. I entered Dido. Surprisingly, the place was busy for a Monday. I realized that it must be the cricket match that was on. Dido was deafening when a match was being telecast. I left my helmet with the bartender, who knew me a little. He smiled and directed me to an inside seating, where Steve was. As I walked in, I realized that I had forgotten to fix my hair and now I had no time to do it quickly. As I pushed the door open, my eyes were eagerly looking for him and my heart was racing along merrily. There he was.

As I walked up to him, I could not help noticing that he was not the same guy that I had been thinking about through the day. He was not exactly dressed to kill. I made a quick mental note not to get myself all excited like that. It only ended in disappointment.

"Hi Meera." He shook hands with me. I could see that the incident had intimidated him. Darn! Had I just shut up and kissed him that evening at the party, we would have been a couple celebrating our first anniversary, soon.

"Hey Steve! So, how is the Goa-returned boy doing?"

Soon, we were laughing and talking again. All the good old times were back. Our meetings became more regular. We were proclaimed lovers. There were no inhibitions. Everything just fell right into place. I had started to like Steve, very much. Steve, my love, my soul, my... hic!

ACHA

"Meera, I want to talk to you."

Acha wanted to talk to me! That didn't sound too good. He never wanted to talk to me. I tried not to guess what it was all about.

"Yes, *acha*." I followed him to the garden.

"I was not planning to bring this up, but then your mother left me no option. Why did you ask *amma* not to lookout for a match for you?" *Acha* looked as stern as he sounded.

Oh! So that was it! The topic had surfaced again and this time it was coming straight from the horse's mouth.

"*Acha*…"

"Meera, under no circumstances am I going to allow a Christian boy to be part of the family. One of my daughters has already put me through enough shame and disappointment to last me a lifetime! I will not allow the second one to do the same. You are free to do whatever you like, but not with my consent. You can walk out of the house. We will not get in the way of your life… and we expect you not to try and change our beliefs and way of life either." He did not even look at me after that. I stood there, envying the plants that were getting all his attention. He didn't look at me even once!

I continued to stand there, speechless. Had daddy really said all that I thought I heard him say! Many a times I had imagined

70

breaking the 'Steve' topic to the family and then having to deal with an 'all hell breaks loose' situation at home. But this came to me as a shock. Daddy had obviously meant every word that he had just uttered. I thought of how Nikki had fought her way to marrying the guy of her choice. She had remained as patient as a saint for four years and finally her perseverance had paid off. I was not sure if I had that kind of strength to fight my family.

I silently rode to work.

Acha knows about Steve! Darn! However hard I try to keep it under the lid, it simply doesn't work. They have a way of finding out. Daddy is way smarter than I thought! I am sure that amma might not even have guessed why I had asked her not to look out for boys for me.

Caste differences were beyond me. I simply could not get married the arranged way and I wanted my parents to understand that. And, by the way, what was the big hurry? I could wait.

The silence within me seemed to spread to my surroundings. Everything around me turned quiet. I did not complain about the slow moving traffic. I was not annoyed with the clients. Bakshi did not sound like a jerk.

And then, Nikki called...

"Meera, *acha* was furious when I spoke to him. He has known about this for quite some time now. He only decided to confront you when your late night calls kept getting longer."

Nikki was clearly not on my side. She did not support my case nor did she understand me the way I had when she first told me about Amit.

"You are being very immature, Meera. Everything seems rosy at first, but once you start living together under the same roof, it all starts falling apart. For God 's sake, he is a Christian! We are so different...two entirely different kind of people. These reasons may sound trivial to you right now, but trust me they are good enough to break a marriage. Look at your brother-in-law. What a great boyfriend he was! But as a husband, he sucks! Sometimes I wonder if he is having an affair. The only good things that happened to us are our children. I know that he will come back home for them, if not for me."

Where was this heading? I had to interrupt her.

"Nikki, stop! Steve is not like that. He is a great guy. I don't want to get married to a stranger. Come on! You should be doing all the talking to *acha* for me. I thought you would understand me better than anyone else."

"No, I don't understand. You figure it out and talk to *amma* and *acha*. I am not calling you again to talk about this, Meera. I don't want to get involved." Nikki cut the call.

That was mean. It was easy for Nikki to wash her hands off the entire affair, but what about me! I knew that I had not been exactly great when it came to taking decisions in life, but, in this case, they simply had to trust me!

I had a sinking feeling that troubled times were looming ahead.

Ten minutes after I got off the phone with Nikki, Steve called.

"Steve, I want to meet you now."

"Hey! What happened? Let us meet at seven." Steve sounded anxious.

I was at a point where the slightest disagreement would have me flying off the handle. The quietness around me had vanished. I would be dead by seven! Why couldn't he understand that I was upset? Steve was never sensitive to my emotions! He kissed me when I didn't want to. Then, when I felt comfortable enough to make the move, he spoiled it all by passing a sarcastic comment. Now, my being upset did not even bother him! He had work!

"Steve, can we meet now?" I tried my best to keep my cool, but one wrong word from him would have blown my fuse off.

"Baby, I have to stay around till six. I will try and leave early but I am not sure," he said.

The fuse blew. "No Steve, you know what, let us not meet today. I am just not in a great mood. I have to hang up. Bye!"

This was not good. I knew I was behaving badly, again, but I didn't care. I let Steve worry. I did not answer his calls or messages for the rest of the day. Was it Nikki's call that had upset me or was it Steve's attitude? I didn't know.

We spoke later. Rather, we fought later. But it did not last very long. I wanted to meet him and so we did. But things changed over the next few days. The physical intimacy was leading to a feeling of guilt. We were talking, but on entirely different lines. I was no longer listening to the mundane office talks of his and he was barely putting up with my stories. Soon, we were deliberating whether we should be meeting once in a while rather than regularly. I had started avoiding Steve's calls altogether at home.

Things at home had also begun to change. There were no more of those speeches from *amma*. also She did not question me anymore about coming home late.

Nikki started coming home with the kids more often. I looked forward to spending time with Manu and Paru. I also started staying over at Nikki's when bro-in-law went out of town. Paru, especially, was growing very fond of me. She never left my side when I was around. While my girlfriend skills were clearly on the wane, my motherly instincts were growing exponentially!

At home, I always stayed locked in my room. I was an emotional wreck at times, who could sob through the funniest of movies! I was missing something. Was it Steve? Or was I upset because daddy was not the same anymore? We had not been very close to each other, but he had never 'hated' me. And now, he would walk out of the room if I was around. We no longer had dinner together. There was a big disconnect with Steve. There was a bigger disconnect with *acha*. Steve liked me. But had I stopped liking him? If *Acha* had not talked to me the other day, everything would have been fine.

I stayed awake for a long time, most nights. My turbulent thoughts overpowered my sleep. I was praying that this phase would be short lived.

SO, SHOULD WE CALL OUR
RELATIONSHIP OFF?

Although my love life had taken a back seat, my career had begun to shine. I had met my targets in the previous three quarters. When the results were announced, my name was flashing in every email, with various variants of 'top performer' being the subject line. In the second quarter, Sanjay and Bakshi promised me that elusive promotion…provided…and here was the catch…provided I stayed consistent for the next two quarters. I knew that this was nothing more than the proverbial 'carrot' to keep the mule running. The pseudo promises no longer interested me. Funnily enough, whenever he saw me disturbed, Sanjay kept making the same promise over and over again. "I asked Bakshi to get the letter ready. The guy never gives it on time. Let me go and check." Then, he would walk away with a 'I-know-I-can-get-away-with-it' wink. Sanjay's jokes and wisecracks were beginning to tire me. I was also avoiding Sri and Charu.

"Meera, what is happening? You have to tell us. Is it Steve? See, I told you that he is not a nice guy. Just the other day, I was enquiring about him through Ansh's friend. He told me that Steve is moody. He does not mingle with everyone. You should be careful with guys who do not talk much. They can be very harmful." Charu sounded concerned.

"You know, when I first saw him at your party, I thought he was gay! Did you notice that he had shaved his chest? Oops!

Meera…sorry…that just kind of slipped out…you are not seeing him anymore, are you?" How typical of Sri to simply blurt out something and then pretend to be all apologetic about it! I had heard about people not thinking twice about what they said, but this girl didn't even think once! Oh, and she thinks I am not seeing him? Sometimes, friends are worse than enemies! You cannot even dump them, especially if they have grown quite close to you. Hmmm, on second thoughts, maybe it was a good thing to find out what they really thought of Steve.

So, Sri had been looking at Steve's chest! Well, I had not noticed the chest hair, or the lack thereof, that evening. The lights had been quite dim. So, all that while when she had been pretending to be busy with Deepak, she had actually been staring at chests she had no business to be staring at! And, how does having no chest hair make someone gay? It is just that it doesn't grow all that much.

They were having a happy conversation, while I was having a tough time biting through the sandwich.

"Steve, mom wants to go out today. I can't come. I am sorry." Of late, our conversations had been reduced to just messages and the occasional displeasing phone calls.

"It has been two weeks, Meera. I want to see you sweetheart."

The 'sweetheart' was not sounding all that pleasant any more. I didn't really want to hear it.

"Steve. Please try and understand."

"No Meera, I will wait for you at four at Bristo. We have to talk. You can go out with your mom, some other day. Bye." Steve hung up on me.

I was not angry. I just put my phone on silent and stared at the wallpaper on my desktop. My team kept asking me if everything was all right. It took a lot of willpower to smile back and let them know that it was.

So, if he really wanted to, Steve could meet me at four! Wasn't this my chance to say that I had to stick around in office till six? And, he didn't sound gay at all. He sounded very strong…very much like a man when he said, 'We have to talk. You can go out with your mom another day'. I should have been falling for it!

"Meera, is there something that you want to tell me?" Steve was bloody serious. I had never seen him like that, before.

Yes, there was. I wanted to tell him that I wanted a coffee. But…

"No. There is nothing." I said. "I am just upset with whatever is happening at home. I will be alright."

"It is almost five months now. We do not talk like before. We do not meet at all. Whenever I try to call or meet, you find flimsy excuses to put the phone down or not meet. We are behaving like strangers. What should we be doing next, Meera? You have to tell me."

He punctuated his sentences by occasionally banging his palm down on the table. I hate it when someone does that and especially if that someone happens to be with me. But this time, I was not reacting to it.

"Yeah, things at home have changed. I try to keep myself happy but I am not able to." I said.

"What about me, Meera? You are no longer even thinking about us. So what if your father is angry with you? You can't ignore us. We are the pair." Steve was angry.

"Shouldn't I be upset, if dad is upset with me?"

"I am not saying no…but he will talk to you eventually. You need to give more time to our relationship. These fights with our folks are bound to happen. You cannot let our love drift because of something that happens at home!" Steve said.

"My mind is too worked up. I cannot think of two different things right now," I said.

"So, what is on your mind? That is what I want to know," he said.

"I told you. It is all about what is happening at home," I said, wanting desperately to end the argument.

'"Okay. So should we call our relationship off?" He stared at me.

"I didn't say that! Why are you assuming things?" I could not even look at his face.

"Okay. So you want us to be together?" Steve was not going to give up so easily.

"Yeah! But right now my head is too muddled up." I looked away.

"And the reason is your home." He looked away too.

For the last five months, I had not been involved in such a long discussion. My hands were shaking. I hated to see Steve like that. He was not the same guy. Maybe Charu was right. He was a 'not-so-very-open-minded-guy' and, right then, that 'not-so-very-open-minded guy' was not behaving nicely. I kept staring through the glass pane at a table beyond it, until I saw the guy sitting at the table smiling back at me! Then, I quickly shifted my focus to my coffee and occasionally to Steve. Steve was still angry.

"Do you love me, Meera?" Steve asked, rather abruptly

"What are you asking?" I had been dreading this very question.

"It is not a very difficult question at all, Meera."

"I don't understand why we need to talk about this now!" Catching the eye of a passing waiter, I indicated that I needed the menu.

"You don't love me." Steve sounded miserable.

"You are mad. Of course, I like you. Happy?" I stole a quick glance at him, when he turned to call the waiter.

"Excuse me. Can you please get us the check?" Steve was not talking any more. He was going to leave.

"What did I say now, Steve? Was it wrong? Tell me something. Please don't just walk away without even talking to me!" I tried to stop him.

"Should I be telling you? You know it all, Meera. Your love for me is just falling off. I kept consoling myself thinking that you still like me...but that is not the case. I should have seen it earlier. But, it really is never too late. We will keep in touch. Take care." And he was gone! The bill was paid. The table was cleared... and so was the load of love!

When I reached home, Vittal *acha* was already there. We spoke briefly. I could just not have my dinner. I was desperately trying to reach out to Steve. Not that I wanted him back...I just wanted to talk to him. However, my messages were unanswered. Steve was gone! I made one final attempt, messaging 'I love you'...but the timing was wrong, perhaps. No reply at all.

Just when I had put my phone away and tears were welling up in my eyes, *acha* and *amma* came into the room. *Amma* stood near the door. Daddy came up to me "Are you alright? Why are you crying?" He sounded bothered, but not very anxious at all.

"No, it is about work. I processed a wrong order and my manager screamed at me." I wiped my tears off.

"Are things going to be fine?" *Acha* asked.

"Yes, *Acha*."

Acha did not waste time. He continued. "Vittal was here for a reason. He has found a suitable proposal for you. The boy's parents want to meet you. I want to know your decision. Shall we ask them to come home?"

I wish *acha* had been around when I told Steve that I could not handle two different things at a time! Why was this happening to me? Did God find no one other than me to burden with troubles?

"*Acha*, I am not ready now. Can we talk about it later? It is not about Steve. The reason is that I am not ready for marriage."

"They are just coming over to meet you," *acha* said.

" Please *acha*.."

Acha stopped me. "If it is not about that guy, then why are you refusing to meet someone else? We are your parents. We will only do what is good for you. Your *amma* and I will be happy if you agree to meet them."

Did daddy just say that he would be happy? Did that mean he would talk to me? If that was the case, my answer was going to be easy.

"Okay *acha*. I will meet them."

ARRANGED MEETINGS

The Vittal *acha*-initiated proposal never came home, but there were several others that did. We had a steady stream of visitors over the next two months. It felt as if our community constituted about half the population of Bangalore! I even set a new benchmark for the girls in our extended *Palakkadan* family by meeting three boys in a single day!

I was quite amused to note how important a role superstitions played in deciding the outcomes of these meetings. While dad could find no fault with the bank manager's proposal, *achamma* snubbed it for a very curious reason. "*Da* Madhu, the boy came to meet her on a Thursday. Thursday unlucky *alle*? It is the day for losses. I will not approve this boy for Meera." I was more than happy to concur with grandma on this one. 'Thursday for losses', 'Saturday for no luck', '*Rahukalam*', '*Chova Dosham*'. I simply loved my grandma and her irrational rationales!

Bank Manager! *Acha* was not even inviting anyone remotely cool.

Home Team: *Acha, Amma, Achamma*, Vittal *Acha*, Nikki, Amit, Manu, Paru and me

Away Team: Boy (mostly)

Venue: The Madhav Residence

The unfortunate boys who came over were scrutinized to pieces, as if they were some disease-causing bacteria that needed to be investigated thoroughly. While all prospective grooms, without bias, had to portray a convincing image, those that could boast of ancestors who had left distinctive marks in history had a definite edge. To one particular boy, *achamma* said, "So you are *Alathur* Tahsildar Sasidharan's grandson." Then, with scant regard for the boy's presence, she whispered aloud to my dad and Vittal *acha* "He comes from a good family. I know them." Whispering about the boys right in front of them should have been a good enough reason for them to reject us but for some odd reason the grand jury never had to put up with a case of rejection.

Some of the rejected candidates simply refused to fade away into oblivion. A few of them kept coming back to *acha* and Vittal *acha*, as if the passage of time would have somehow improved their odds of getting a favorable response. The complexity of this arranged marriage circus was simply beyond me!

Like in reality shows, eliminations happened at various stages. The first round of rejection happened at *acha*'s rank. Contestants that made past this round faced the formidable duo of Vittal *acha* and *achamma* in round two. Also, like in reality shows, there were rules. Only, in this case, the poor contestants were not aware of them. Nevertheless, they were still expected to adhere to the rules.

a. Never initiate a conversation with elders. They ask and you answer. Period.

b. When the question is in Malayalam, make sure you reply in the same language.

c. Do not appear to be very comfortable in your seat. Show signs of nervousness. Vittal *acha* was the best judge on this aspect. If the boy looked more relaxed than was acceptable, he would immediately interpret it as '*ahankaram*' (excessive pride) and walk out of the room. This was a clear sign to the home team not to waste time anymore.

In short, the contestants were judged mainly using the 'Rule-of-the-three-S', as I liked to call it. In the order of importance, these desirable traits were smile, speech and simplicity, all mixed in just the right proportion.

Nikki and I found these two months greatly amusing. After the boys left, and despite the fact that they were rejected, I would invariably have to suffer through a 'grilling' session. "Meera, you looked only half interested. The only reason we even bothered to meet this boy was because we care for you. But if you are not happy, then we are all wasting our time." That was *achamma*. I bought her line of reasoning. I was not interested, definitely. But for the life of me I could not understand how I had managed to look 'half interested' when I had not even been allowed to come out of my room!

"How can you judge a boy by just looking at his photo? You should meet him to know him well, right? I know that you have already made up your mind to say 'No'. This attitude will get you nowhere." That was *amma* playing doomsday prophet.

I kept hearing various versions of the same set of words for most of the two months. *Acha* did not talk to me about my disinterest or attitude, ever. Nikki laughed with me through the meetings but then stood by *amma*'s side through my pre-marriage counseling sessions.

Arranged Meeting 1

"Where in Kerala are your parents from?"

"I am not sure uncle. It is a place called Mo...Hmmm... I am not very sure." The poor, confused boy was smiling expectantly even as my folks conveyed their verdict to one another with grave shakes of their heads.

REJECTED.

Arranged Meeting 8

"*Meira*, why don't you sit? I ain't no stranger, y'know. We gotta be good friends b'fore we can hook up, y'know…so no formalities." That was the cool dude from the States, who was in India on vacation. He had barely been abroad for a year, but had managed to pick a typical Indo-American expat accent. Nikki was biting her lips and pinching herself not to burst out laughing. *Achamma* and Vittal *acha* pronounced the guy guilty of violating rule 'c'.

REJECTED.

Arranged Meeting 13

"I have a confession to make. My job demands a lot of travelling and so I occasionally eat non-vegetarian food…because the places I go to leave me with very little choice, you see."

I did see. Honestly. But I also did see Vittal *acha*'s eyes popping out of their sockets in disbelief in response to this confession. He smirked and left the room, a clear sign that I was to end the conversation as soon as possible.

REJECTED.

Arranged Meeting 21

The family accompanied the boy. His parents were talking to mine, while I was allowed to talk to the boy in my room.

"So, you are a sales executive?" he asked.

"Sales account manager, actually," I answered, curtly.

"My mother told me that you are very religious."

Really? While I do admit to having my share of faults, nobody could ever accuse me of being religious! So he wants a typical, religious and homely girl, does he? Alright, Meera, time to fulfill his wish!

The degree of curtness went up one notch. "No, I am hardly religious. Is that a problem?"

"No, I just asked. It doesn't matter. So can you cook?"

Ah, how predictable! I knew that this question was coming.

Was this guy for real! He seemed to have been born a century too late!

"I could boil eggs, I guess. But in our community we are not even allowed to do that. So, does that answer your question?" I stared at him with defiant eyes.

The boy was not interested. I could see that. For a change, Mr. Madhav and family were going to be rejected.

"What do you like doing when you are not working? Do you go out often? Do you have many friends?" He was desperately trying to make a late come back.

But I was all set to snub this late rally. With deliberate politeness, I replied. "I definitely go out on weekends…and most week days, too. I spend a lot of time with my friends. I have many in Bangalore. You can hardly find me at home. I love to party. I come home late. I am a shopaholic. I don't have much of savings. I am not a homely person. I hate visiting relatives. I am short tempered and don't get along with people that well."

That is it! I knew that the guy was never going to come back. As I watched him quietly sipping the coffee, I couldn't help but feel victorious. I looked at Vittal *acha* in the living room. He signaled to me that the boy's family was great. Little did he know that the boy was forming the exact opposite opinion about me at that very moment.

The family left. I imagined the boy's plight on his way back home. *Achamma* came up to me "How did you like the boy?" This time I pretended to look interested, knowing fully well that it was safe to do so. "*Achamma*, I think he is ok."

"My good girl, Meera." *Achamma* could not have sounded happier. My family could not have looked happier. A tendril of guilt crept across my heart. I hoped that the boy would simply reject me without telling his family about the little conversation we had.

I had often caught myself thinking about Steve during these

arranged meetings. I was missing him. I had tried to call and message him, but Steve had never answered. I sent him one more message "*Hey baby! I am really sorry for what happened. I want to meet you. I want to talk to you. Please reply.*"

I was in my room. I was upset, again. My head was buried in my pillow when a message beeped on my phone. "*Meera, I miss you too. But it is best that we don't get back together. You don't love me anymore. Let us not meet. Bye.*"

How did he even decide that I did not love him anymore? Steve sounded so rude. I cried and stayed in my room for a long time. My messages and calls had made no difference to Steve. He was gone…long gone.

"They said yes. They have invited us home this weekend."

Oh my god! How could this have happened? I stepped out of the room to check if I had heard *acha* right. I knew at once that my worst fears had come true. The Madhav residence was the scene of one happy celebration! Everybody was deliriously happy and chattering away. Nikki was busy offering sweets to *achamma* and Vittal *acha*. Manu and Paru were jumping up to reach the plate that Nikki was holding and she was mock warning them not to eat too many. Seeing me, she happily urged the kids to kiss me for the good news.

Even as I stood there in a dazed state, Vittal *acha* and *achamma* left home promising that they would announce it to the entire family. As soon as they left, I turned to *amma* and blurted out, "I don't want to get married. I am very sure about it. Please call them and say no."

Before anyone could react, I dashed into my room and shut the door. I could not face the questions that were sure to follow. Nikki knocked on the door several times and even tried calling me on my phone. As a last resort, she asked Manu and Paru to call out to me, but I dared not step out of the room. When the attempts stopped, I knew that she had left for her home. I was glad that Amit had not been around to see the drama.

When I could no longer stay in my room, I hesitantly stepped out and went to the kitchen to get some food. Bad move!

"Meera, what is the problem? We started to look out for an alliance with your consent. You agreed to this boy a while ago. Why is it that you changed your opinion within an hour's time? Is it that boy? Are you still meeting him?"

"*Acha*, I am sorry that I said yes a while ago. But that is not what I had in mind. I don't want to get married. I did not like the guy. I just…"

"You thought that you could waste our time? My mother and brother have been here most weekends, meeting people, enquiring about them and when they finally find you a good match, you behave like this? So indifferent? Vittal has already given the good news to our people here and in Palakkad. I know that this does not make any difference to you." *Acha* was standing right at the entrance to the kitchen. I could neither escape to my room nor face him. Darn! I should have said no when *achamma* asked me.

"*Acha*, the boy wanted to know if I could cook and if I go to temples regularly. Is that all he is interested in? How can I live with someone who is so unlike me? It is almost as if we speak two entirely different languages!"

"I am sure you must have told him that you cannot cook and that you are not very religious. He still came back to you because he knows that these are petty issues. But my princess feels that she deserves a man from another planet!" Daddy was warming up and his animated expressions were beginning to surface.

"You are going to break many hearts, Meera. *Achamma* was looking forward to Nikki's marriage but she disappointed her. This is your chance to make her happy but you will not. I am an unlucky father! Both my daughters have let me down. How will I ever face my people? I had a lot of hope from you, but you are no different. You are giving me a lot of pain, Meera."

Acha sat down on a chair with his head in his hands as if to say, "*What the hell have I done to deserve this?*" I had seen this reaction many times before, through all the sessions my parents had with Nikki when she had been trying to convince them for Amit. I could not figure out how the current situation compared to Nikki's case, but the reactions were the same. *Acha* was now slowly rubbing his chest. *Amma* ran to console him. He refused the glass of water she offered, all the time looking at her as if hinting that it was all over.

"*Acha*, what wrong have I done? It is just that I don't want to get married to this boy. I am ready to meet others."

A furious *amma* turned to glare at me. "Do you think that this is some kind of joke? You may find it amusing to continue meeting other boys, but we know when to stop our search. The family, the boy and his job are faultless. We thought that this was best for you. Do what you like, Meera!"

"*Amma*, aren't you bothered about me? Don't you want me to be happy? I am not going to be happy with him. I want you to…"

Daddy got up from his chair, "Meera do as you like. You want me to meet that Christian boy? I will definitely meet him. We will not stop you." He just walked to the bedroom. I watched mother sniff and sob into her saree.

I could not sleep that night. I could hear *acha* and *amma* tossing and turning in their room and talking in low whispers. They could not asleep, either. What had I gotten my family into?

Next morning, I got ready to go to office. I saw daddy sitting on the sofa, staring fixedly at a point on the floor. He was not reading his newspaper or spending time in the garden, as he usually did at that time of the day. My heart broke to see him so unhappy and hurt.

"*Acha*, I am sorry. I am ready for the marriage. You can talk to them." I had made up my mind and knew what I was saying. At that point, my daddy was the most important person in my life.

"It is alright, Meera. I don't want to force you into anything. All parents want their children to be happy and if you are not then we don't want to go ahead." All the while, daddy kept staring at that spot. Clearly, he didn't want to look at me. He was restless.

"No *acha*. I know that you want the best in life for me. I have really thought this over. I will not change my mind again. I am ready," I said.

"No, Meera. I don't want to make a promise to someone and then break it," acha said. "We will be called fickle. I don't want to be laughed at by others."

"*Acha*, please. I will not change my mind again. I am saying this with all my heart."

Acha sat back on the sofa, looking very pale and stern at the same time. He pointed his finger at me. "Is this your final decision? Did you really think it over? Can I give them my word?"

I tried hard not to think about the boy. I had to sound confident...happy. "Yes *acha*." I think I said it exactly like he wanted me to.

Acha got up and left the room to talk to *amma* in the kitchen. I looked at *amma* and smiled a little, hoping to comfort her. Whenever I thought too hard about things that I did not like, I got worked up. The solution was to focus on things around me. I was having breakfast. I forced myself to concentrate on the cornflakes and milk.

"Geetha, what is the boy's name?" Did *acha* have to remind me of something unpleasant?

"Vineet!"

LAST FEW DAYS AS MS. MEERA

I stood there…confused…hoping against hope that somehow a miracle would happen and the marriage would be called off.

The celebration, a three-day long affair, was the biggest in my family in living memory. Aunts and uncles had all planned their leaves and flight schedules to make it to my wedding. I found myself bestowing half-hearted smiles at relatives, some of whom I did not even recognize. Though my house was packed with relatives, everyone ensured that my room was relatively free. I was treated lavishly to gifts, jewelry and praise. After every drink, Prabhu *mama* from Dubai would saunter in to say something nice about me. "Meera *kutty* has always been my favorite. She is well educated…has a good job. But you know what's most important? She is a very obedient girl who is getting married according to her parents' wish. What more can a father ask for?" Saying this he would glare at Parvati, his daughter, who had only recently announced her love for someone…in fact, just days before their trip to India. That partly explained *mama's* exaggerated drinking spree! I wonder what he would have thought had he known about the high drama that had nearly rocked the Madhav residence three months earlier. *Acha* seemed only happy to concur with *mama* and was nodding in agreement to the lavish praises being bestowed upon his daughter. It seemed like I was the only one in my family who remembered the chain of events triggered by

Vineet's first visit to our house.

Nikki, being the active element in the family, emerged as a successful event coordinator. She had worked out the plans for a 'traditional-yet-modern' wedding to the minutest detail. The theme for each day, parties, dances, dramas (scripted dramas, courtesy my cousins, and real-life dramas, thanks to my aunts and uncles. The latter type is also called 'family dramas' and are a regular feature whenever over-the-top extended families, such as mine, get together and old issues are raked up). The synchronized clothing she organized for men, women, girls, boys and kids was flawless.

The highlighted event was definitely the pre-marriage bridal photo shoot. This event inevitably brings out the non-existing, highly pretentious, 'deep' love between cousins. The videographer is the undisputed boss during this event. Even the bride's father defers to this awesome specimen of mankind. Under his directions, I found myself boxed between various combinations of relatives. One combination consisted of an aunt, the corresponding uncle and their children. Another of this same aunt and her co-sisters (who invited them in the first place?). A third combination was of appropriate pairs picked from the vast pool of aunts and uncles.

The cousins were intolerable. Their pose for most photos consisted of a plastic smile and an expression that advertised a 'perfect, nice girl' image. They stood with their hands locked below their waists, slightly tilted to their right and with necks held stiff so as not to spoil their hairdo. A pain crept into my neck as I watched them. I was even asked to step out of the frame while they had their individual photos snapped. Narcissism often overpowered their love for me! When the shoot was done, or rather when the photographer had nearly collapsed from exhaustion, each of them walked up to me and said, "Chechi, tag me on Facebook, ok?"

Achamma and Vittal *acha* were my pillars of strength during all this fun and frolic. They kept checking on me to see if I was all right. Vittal *acha* came up to me and asked if there was anything bothering me. He had guessed that something had gone wrong after he had left my house the day Vineet had first come to see me. I had honestly tried my best to remain happy, but my face said it all, I guess.

"Ask Meera to stay cheerful. Vittal has been asking me if she was forced into the marriage."

Until then I had an irrational and extremely foolish hope that *acha* would call off the wedding. But I realized that nothing could change now. To save him from embarrassment, I would have to show to the world that I was very kicked about the wedding. *Amma* delivered this message of his and shed a few tears to reinforce the idea that I had better put up a more convincing performance before the rest of the family started asking the same question. But Vittal *acha* was not convinced.

He came to me, "Meera, my dear, are you happy?"

"Yes *acha*, I am fine." I don't think that sounded very convincing.

"I spoke to the boy's parents the other day, but not to the boy." Vittal *acha* said. "The reason being you told us that you liked him. Now to think of it, I should have."

"No *acha*. Don't bother. No one is forcing me into marrying him. He is fine." I think I only said that because I had to comfort him.

"Did you both meet anytime?" he asked.

"Yes, we did. Once."

"What did he say?"

"We did not speak much." I replied. "It was mostly about my work. He told me that I didn't have to continue working after marriage. I could quit if I wanted to."

"Did he say that? That is not right. Never stop working, Meera, unless there is a very compelling reason to quit." The tone of his voice clearly revealed that Vittal *acha* was worried.

"I told him the same. I am not going to stop working, ever."

"Now I understand. He is different from you. But, these are very insignificant issues. Do not let it affect you. I have enquired about the family and the boy with my friends. They all said that you are very lucky to be a part of Mr. Hariharan's family. They don't know much about the boy, but they are sure that the family is really good." Saying this Vittal *acha* walked away.

That was comforting. I smiled whole heartedly for the first time in three months. Vittal *acha* kept calling his friends to know more about Vineet. I wished then that I had told Vittal *acha* about my disinterest towards this marriage as soon as Vineet had agreed to it. He would have stood by me for sure. Or would he? After all, he was Mr. Madhav's brother, wasn't he? How different could he be? I could never have been sure of his support.

Vittal *acha*'s phone calls and inquiries were not going to help me much. The marriage was to take place in two days. I was advised to take enough rest.

"Sleep well. Don't let the tiredness show on your face. I had dark circles on the day of my wedding. Can you imagine?" That was Nimmi, my first cousin, who is younger to me by two years. She has ever been a nemesis and one of the main reasons why I was going through this suffering. She got married at a young age because there was nothing much that she was planning to do with her life. She did not want to work nor did she want to study beyond her twelfth standard. After she went through many unsuccessful attempts to pass the exam, her father gave up hope and arranged a marriage for her. To add to the pain, she had gone ahead and promptly got pregnant! When the news about her pregnancy leaked out in the family, it was as if a bomb had been dropped on the Madhav household. My life had become a living hell for a long time after that. Now, Nimmi's aim in life was to have a beautiful son like Nikki's Manu. Right from her childhood, Nimmi had always looked up to Nikki. So much so that she even went to the extent of getting her name changed from Janaki to Nimmita. I am not sure if the name has any meaning. But it rightfully belongs to a Malayalee! Come to think of it, Nimmita is way better than Litti, Mosi, Gigi, Prento and other such Malayalee names that are abominable combinations of the names of the bearer's parents.

The day before the wedding was straight out of a horror movie. My head reeled as I watched the sea of guests who had flooded our house. The visitors were interested mostly in seeing the jewelry and saris that I had inherited by agreeing to this deal (What else do you call an arrangement that involves trading my independence and ideals in return for materialistic gifts? Oh, I know… Big Deal!). I did not have many saris, but Nikki quickly stacked up a few of her own to display to the spectators. This bit of deception was necessary, I was given to understand. 'To stop tongues from wagging,' as Nikki 'know-all' informed me later.

My aunts and mom took it upon themselves to educate me about some 'obligations' associated with the social contract that I was going to enter into the next day. They went to the extent of asking me not to get jittery on the first night, but to stay calm and let him perform the 'act', if he so desired. The sex education was initiated by Latha *Maami*, who dropped subtle hints that she was the ultimate authority on that matter. I so wanted to ask her to read my blog, *The Boobie Obsession*, and react with any questions that she might have.

If the day was horrible, the night was no better. I had occasional bouts of panic attack and could not sleep for a long time. And just as I was beginning to get some sleep, *amma* and the legion of aunties woke me up.

Why do South Indian weddings demand early morning rituals? I had been given a traditional turmeric bath the previous day and on the day of the wedding, my aunts took turns to drench me in milk. The way some of them dumped the milk on me made me suspect that their acts were pre-planned and vengeful, rather than dictated by pious traditional motives. I must say that the milk bath felt a lot better than the astronomically expensive bridal spa treatment I had subjected myself to at that parlor the other day!

I had to rush through my bath, as I was not permitted to have an elaborate one. No one really bothered to understand my need to spend time with my private space...my room...my bathroom...as I was not going to come back there the next day. As I came out, my aunts and cousins were waiting in my room to drape the sari around me. I was told that this was another (pointless) ritual. But with just the towel wrapped around me, how was I going to wear my essentials? While they were still busy showing off their expensive clothes to one another, I quickly wore these less expensive, but more vital items of clothing with Nikki's help. Soon I was dressed up. My makeup lady gave me a slight composition of color that I thought was perfect but was met with the general disapproval of all my cousins. While one thought the cheekbones had to be highlighted a little more, another felt the acute need to sharpen my nose. I only smiled at them and walked out of the room as I had better things to worry about.

Acha, amma, Vittal *acha* and *achamma* were among the few elders who were genuinely happy that day. It was pleasant to watch the decorations at home. It made me cheerful despite the fact that what was to follow would snuff all the joy out of my life. That apart, the most important reason to stay cheerful was to see my family smiling. It made me happy enough to smile for all the photos taken. The smile was nothing compared to the artificial ones my cousins had been sporting for the best part of three days. Even before they could say anything, I assured them "I will tag your pictures, definitely."

The groom and his family arrived at the *Kalyana Mantap*

just after we did. The rituals began. It was a long process. I was hoping against hope to see Steve. I had invited him but he was nowhere to be seen. Why would he come? But wait! Could he have messaged me? I quickly got hold of my phone, which had been stashed away in one of the aunts' bags. "*Dearest Meera, I wish you a happy married life. Cheers, Steve.*" Steve remembered, but there was clearly no love anymore. The message brought back the same depression that had loomed over me when I used to stay locked in my room. I could not afford to cry with all the makeup on and people around.

Sri and Charu made it to the wedding with their husbands. They came straight to the green room. We kept talking through the lengthy rituals that involved only the groom. They had always wanted to be introduced to my fiancé, but I had successfully thwarted them so far. Sri held my hand "Meera, will you at least introduce us to him today?" Like I had an option!

I was summoned to the *Mantap*. I did not look at Vineet. People who watched me go around the decorated tomb and witnessed my momentary composure would have mistaken me for a girl blessed with oodles of obedience and modesty. Vineet's parents kissed me on my forehead and gently touched my head when I sought their blessings. Vittal *acha* was so right. Mr. and Mrs. Hariharan were really nice people. I was then asked to sit next to Vineet, who was busy pouring ghee into the fire. I glanced at him out of the corner of my eye. He tried to initiate a conversation, but I just smiled to ignore the gesture. I was hoping that someone would dramatically walk into the hall, point an accusing finger at Vineet and claim that he was the father of her unborn child. I imagined how the ghee would freeze in mid air as it trickled from the spoon.

There were a lot of thoughts running in my mind then. I went back to the night when I had the argument with *acha*. Had I not bothered about hurting him, I would have been single and happy. At this time, I would be getting ready to go to work. Paru and

Manu were running around in the hall with the other children. I wished I was on the other side of the hall as a guest only.

None of my prayers were answered.

A change of music by the *Melam* (a small band) boys signified a change in my status from 'Single' to 'Complicated'. I had entered wedlock. There was a three-inch wide pendant strung to a turmeric-coated thread hanging around my neck. It did not look great.

I was Mrs. Meera Vineet!

I hoped to quickly come to terms with this unpleasant marriage.

VINEET HARIHARAN

It was a pleasure getting to know Vineet's parents. Even though I missed my parents a lot, it was nice to be with a family that welcomed me as one of their own. Over the next few days, my in-laws went out of their way to make me comfortable. Vineet's father would often drop me off at the office and even volunteer to pick me up after work. Vineet's mother was nice enough in her own way. She insisted that I carry lunch to work and, unlike other mothers-in-law, never complained about my incompetence at household chores.

Our room was pretty much the only thing that Vineet and I shared in common. I could not even bring myself to look at his face for any length of time. His proximity made me uncomfortable to the extent that I felt it would strangle the love I felt for his parents. Before marriage, I had always imagined that I would have to suffer the wrath of my in-laws for coming home late from work. But soon I realized that my 'in-times' were very reasonable in comparison to Vineet. I used to look for places to hide when I heard the doorbell ring at that time of the evening when he usually came home. The kitchen was not a great hideout at all. "Meera, it must be Vineet. Get the door, ma". Vineet's mother was just too polite to be ignored.

The tension between us or rather the 'unlove' within me was there for all to see. Is 'unlove' even a word? It seems to convey my feelings, or the lack thereof, so well! His concerned parents tried their best to bring us closer. They even arranged a trip to relieve the awkwardness that they thought I was feeling. A lot of money was spent in planning the trip, but I pulled out at the last moment, stating some very lame reason, thus derailing the plan and dashing his parents' hopes. I could not help it. I tried my best to stay happy, but the mere sight of Vineet was enough to put me into a state of emotional distress and restlessness.

I was beginning to reconcile to this life when one day, quite out of the blue, Vineet's father made an announcement. "Your mother and I have decided that both of you should move to our flat in Chandranagar. We have arranged everything. All that you guys have to do is pack your luggage and be ready to shift the day after tomorrow." God! I could not believe that this was actually happening. Sure enough, Vineet's face was also contorted in a grimace that hovered somewhere between pain and anger. I knew that I had always had an unfathomable connection with trouble. Trouble was always around the corner, faithfully waiting for me!

I made many conscious and calm attempts to let my in-laws know that I was comfortable and happy at their place. However, my words were disregarded. They insisted that this proposed change of residence was necessary. I talked to Vineet (yes, that was how desperate I was!) to convince his parents to abandon this attempt at bringing us close. However, his attempts to talk them into seeing sense backfired, resulting in an unexpected twist. "I completely missed it! Both of you are not working tomorrow, right? So why wait until the day after? Let us move to your new home tomorrow then." His father walked away with a big smile, having communicated in no uncertain terms this latest plan of action. Vineet also shot out of the room like an arrow, even as I started to fret.

On D- day, I was asked to ride in the front with Vineet. This, of course, was the natural thing to do and could hardly be termed an unusual request. But the fact was that I did not want to be seen riding with Vineet by anyone I knew. Despite being married to him.

"Meera, you can park your bike next to his car in the porch." Vineet's father said.

Was that really important? Did they even know what a big mistake they were committing by setting us adrift? Alone?

"But why does she need to park her bike, anymore? Shouldn't we tell her?" asked Vineet's mother, nudging her husband. What now? Did they have another bit of news up their sleeve? I could not handle surprises anymore, but who could stop the inevitable? I braced myself involuntarily even as my father-in-law prepared to drop the bomb. "Your father wanted us to present you his gift. Your parents have bought you a new car. They tell us that it is your favorite."

I ran outside to see my new possession. A spanking new yellow Alto stood parked on the road, just outside the gate! How had I missed seeing it on the way in? Yay! I had always wanted an Alto… but not a yellow one. But, it was alright. I was not complaining. I wonder when I had told *acha* and *amma* about my desire to have a car. And now I had a car…I had a car!

Vineet let me park the new car in the porch, while willingly parking his own outside the gate. He then unloaded our luggage. I wished that I could simply stand there and admire my car, but all good things have to end and I had to shift focus reluctantly from my brand new machine to our new house. As instructed by Vineet's mother, I entered the place, my 'objectionable' residence, stepping in with my right foot first. She had managed to arrange the pooja room quickly, while I was busy with my 'yellow fever'. We had a quick house-warming ceremony, with the traditional boiling of the milk. This was more for my benefit than for the house itself, since I was new to it. I offered to make tea for my in-laws before they dispersed. The poor guys sipped through the bad-tasting brew without the slightest complaint.

An unexpected thing happened when it was time for my in-laws to leave. Vineet's mother turned to her son, embraced him and burst into tears. The more Vineet tried to comfort her the more she wept in a very strange voice that did not seem like hers at all. In India, it is always the girl's parents who are mentally preparing themselves for this highly emotional ceremony – the daughter's farewell. Since they are constantly preparing themselves, the intensity of the emotions is much subdued when the actual occasion, the girl's wedding, arrives. Tears do flow, but it is not the kind of deluge that one would expect, given our affinity to high drama. It was rather strange to see a mother crying at her son's farewell! Clearly, Vineet's mom had never been prepared to part with her son.

We just let her be. She hugged her twenty-nine year old son several times before finally allowing her husband and son to gently coax her into an auto rickshaw. As I walked back to the apartment, a nagging fear of facing the first few days of this forced living together gnawed at my heart, making me miserable.

Suddenly, I did not want to go in to the house. I didn't care where I went, but I definitely didn't want to go in to the house. Instead, I went around in search of the newspaper vendor, the iron-man (laundry) and explored the stores around. Anything that would allow me to delay the inevitable moment when I would have to entrap myself with Vineet within the four walls of that prison. My delaying tactics could not continue forever, however, and eventually I found myself ringing the doorbell. Vineet opened the door. As always, I did not meet his eyes.

"How do you like our new place?" Vineet asked me.

"It is very nice." I was struggling to unlock my suitcase. Vineet offered to open it for me.

"I bought it in 2007." Vineet said, expertly manipulating the locks. "I wasn't thinking of investing in a flat…I had actually wanted to spend my savings on a new car, perhaps, but definitely not on a flat. It was papa who kept insisting that I invest in real estate. Looks like it is paying off, finally."

I wasn't very sure about that, but I didn't see much of a choice other than to come to terms with my new home.

As I moved towards the wardrobe to place some of my stuff inside, I found Vineet blocking my way. "Meera, why is it that you do not talk to me?" I had always dreaded this question. I really had no answer to it.

"Do you feel that way?" I asked. "Oh! We did not get to know each other well before marriage and I was finding it hard to break the ice between us. That maybe is the reason."

What a convincing answer! I think he bought it, too. I glanced briefly at his face and saw the content spreading across it. This, I think, saved me from further interrogation. "Alright! So let us get to know each other." He turned his attention to unpacking his luggage, while I pretended to be busy in the kitchen, a place where Vineet had no business.

Getting to know each other was no fun. In spite of having been a couple for four months, we had mostly stayed out of each other's way. We began day one in our new apartment by stating out our preferences to each other. This turned out to be more like a listing of our differences than anything else! Day two began with me reversing my new car into one of the pillars of the porch, resulting in a major dent on the right backdoor. My heart broke to see the damage, but I was in no mood to take counseling from a man who had walked into my life just four months ago. We argued briefly.

I also began to appreciate how thoughtless Vineet could be! One evening, about a week after we had moved in, I stepped out of the bathroom and walked into the kitchen only to receive the shock of my life. Standing there and helping himself to a soft drink from my fridge was a total stranger…a mountain of a man! I was about to scream my lungs out when Vineet walked in. "Meera, meet Girish. He missed our wedding." What? So you invite him home without even bothering to let me know? I could only thank my lucky stars that I had been decently clothed while stepping out of the bathroom that day. That was not normally the case, because Vineet was never home at that time of the evening.

I wasn't exactly sure what this Girish had missed the most? Our wedding…or the buffet? Here was a man who had perfected gluttony to an art form. He tucked into the dinner with gusto and spent the next half hour stuffing his face. When he finally left, I could barely hold back my disgust. "You shouldn't spring such shocks on me, Vineet. If you want to invite your health-conscious friend home, at least get him to behave." The fight that followed was mainly over two issues – the use of the term 'health-conscious', which apparently (and actually) reeked of sarcasm and the fact that I had looked as if I was in mourning, rather than the chirpy newlywed that I was supposed to be. I grudgingly conceded a point there. Vineet had successfully maintained a pretentious smile the entire time that Charu and Sri had come visiting that past Sunday. Our quarrels were inevitable and over issues as varied as friends, clothes, jobs, television and my car. My car was a frequent target.

"Why would someone buy a yellow car? You actually like it!" He once asked.

Firstly, the 'someone' in question was my father. Secondly, he had no business judging my color sense. Oh, Mr. Vineet, you are so going to get it!

"Do you have a problem with that?" I snapped. "A guy probably cannot drive a yellow, but a girl can certainly carry it off very well. And, the auto companies are not a bunch of idiots to manufacture a weird-colored car without any ground research."

He never attempted to defend himself. Good! Anyway, on what grounds would he do that? Ignorance? Well, his ignorance was as glaring as his chauvinism, both of which needed to be dealt with in the harshest possible manner.

Our relationship was deteriorating, even as the verbal fights were gaining in intensity. I could not stand the sight of Vineet and I strongly believed that he echoed my sentiments. The only good thing that happened was that we managed to keep our families out of the fights. What to us was just a contract was mistaken as a reasonably good relationship, especially by my parents. Even though Vineet rarely accompanied me on my frequent visits home, *acha* had no clue about how bad things were between us.

On one of the rare occasions that Vineet did come home, he ran into Vittal *acha*. While the rest of my family were big fans of Vineet, Vittal *acha* had been privately harboring misgivings about him. The seeds of doubt had been sown in his mind the day of my wedding, when he had observed me walking to the *mantap* like a sacrificial lamb being led to the altar. He wasn't sure that Vineet was really the nice boy that he and his brother had initially thought him to be.

"How is your work?" Vittal *acha* had initiated that little conversation when my husband was looking all set to bury his head in the newspaper.

"Going well." Vineet replied, sounding far from interested.

"How are you getting along with Meera?" Vittal *acha* persisted.

"Well, you should be asking her that." Vineet said, smiling, as if he had made a very smart comment.

Vittal *acha* did not say anything to him then. He probably did not want to upset things between us. But as he left the room, I could read his thoughts - '*Do you think this is funny?*'

When we came back to our flat after the visit, Vineet brought up his 'confrontation' with Vittal *acha*. I had expected that. But what I had not expected was his question on why I called him *acha*.

My dad's brother had to be ideally called *cheriyacha*, but Vittal *acha* had been very close to Nikki and me since our childhood. He had always been there for us when daddy was away on his business trips. Vineet would never understand the bond I shared with Vittal *acha*. He was raking up the issue simply to irritate me.

Sanjay was another pet peeve for Vineet. There were times during some weekends when Sanjay would call to discuss work. Invariably, the calls would be followed by a zillion questions, courtesy Vineet. The questions were clearly meant to see how close I was to Sanjay. They had the tone of a deeply suspicious, narrow-minded person with no basic ethics. What was surprising was that someone so educated could fall prey to such an acute case of paranoia!

I could not share my feelings with my family or friends. Vineet had become very friendly with Charu and Sri. Why wouldn't he? Would he find better spies than them? One day Sri made a comment about Steve. "Your whirlwind romance with Steve would not have sustained for long. Getting married to him would have been as good as getting married to a stranger...although you had known him for quite some time. You guys were never meant to be. Vineet is any day better than that *firang*." Friends were difficult to ignore at the best of times! I realized that I was not as affected by the remark about Steve as I was by the comparison to Vineet. I had to object to that! I was beginning to realize that my friendship with Sri was turning sour.

With every passing day, it became increasingly clear to me that Vineet had been a mistake. And I had reasons to believe that he was nurturing the same sentiments about me. We fought over almost everything. Our differences definitely caused us trouble. Surprisingly, even the occasional discussions about common interests went off track, leading to huge clashes. Though we had been married hardly a few months, it felt as if we had spent a decade together in mutual disinterest.

SANJAY

I was despairing of waking up every morning in a place to which I did not belong. The despair invariably progressed to trauma by the time I had had my first argument of the day with the only other person living under the same roof. I could hardly remember a day when I left to work without a heavy heart! It was killing me! I was swearing at people while driving. The slightest issue at work induced bouts of anxiety and desperation.

"Hey, look who's here…Junior Bakshi." Though the newest recruit in the team had tried her best to keep her tone hushed, her caustic comment assailed my ears as I walked into my cubicle one day. I wasn't sure if I was meant to react to the comment, because the girl had not said it directly to my face. Secondly, much as I hated to admit it, she was right! I was turning into a Bakshi! Not that my hairline was receding or that I was developing a disgusting beer gut or anything, but I was surely turning into this intimidating monster that all the new recruits were fast learning to avoid. In the larger interest of maintaining office decorum, I refrained from reacting to the comment, then. But I made a mental note of the offender so as to return the favor at the earliest possible opportunity. And I did exactly that by disagreeing with all the points that she ever made during subsequent team meetings. Well, as an established senior I could not be expected to just take smartass comments passed by new kids on the block, however accurate, lying down, could I?

Talking to anyone at home was out of the question. They simply wouldn't understand. I couldn't even bitch to Charu and Sri about Vineet. And if they happened to mention anything positive about the man, I would walk out of the conversation.

I tried my best to keep happy, but things were slipping away. Vineet was turning out to be very difficult to live with. His overall sloppiness, insensitivity and lethargy were exhausting to watch. I looked forward to those occasional blissful moments that I got to spend all alone. I started avoiding going home to *acha* and *amma* because I was getting tired of plastering a happy smile across my face whenever they asked me about Vineet.

I was not good at pleasing my in-laws either. I sucked at doing simple things like calling them up once in a while, treating them to food that I cooked or simply paying them an occasional visit. But, I soon realized that these things would come easily to me if I put my mind to it. Sometimes, Vineet's father would ask us to stay over on weekends. On such occasions, I'd be the first to reach their place. There were times when I was more than happy to drive off to my in-laws even if Vineet was in no mood to go. Vineet's mother tried her hand at introducing me to cooking. Vineet constantly complained that I could not cook. Well, I had warned him about that the day we had first met, hadn't I? So, what was he complaining about now? When he had a chance to reject me on that ground, he had not taken it! Of course, there was no point arguing with him about it. Also, a slight case of food poisoning, caused no doubt by constantly eating from hotels around my office, had made me realize the worth of home-cooked food. Soon, there came a time when I was able to handle cooking two dishes at a time. I even started advising Nikki, the undisputed culinary expert in the family, about the right ingredients for certain dishes and the right time for those ingredients to be added.

What I really needed was to keep myself occupied with

something that I could relate to. Considering that I was now some sort of an expert at cooking, enrolling in a 'cookery class' was not exactly a great option (I wonder what my mom-in-law would have to say had she heard that I had pretensions to being an expert cook!) I asked Nikki, *amma*, Sri, Charu, Amit, Manu and even my two-year old Paru as to what I could do to keep myself occupied. The answers were as varied as the people I polled – dance class, music, foreign language, volunteering for an NGO. My personal favorite was of course Paru's generous offer to let me braid her Barbie's hair, but I could not simply see myself doing that for any fruitful length of time! Amit's answer was like a nail to the heart. "You need to meet new people, sweetheart. You are twenty-seven, but you behave like you are fifty-seven. Hmmm… Actually no! People at sixty are also socializing. You just don't have a life!" Saying so, he walked away without the slightest hint of regret for having ruined my day with that thoughtless statement! Ideally I should have pulled him up and demanded what he meant by that! Of course I went out…just that I could not remember the last time I had done that!

So, the decision was made. I should be going out more often. That gave rise to another question. Who could I go out with?

"Ah, Dido feels good. Thank you, Sanjay." I gulped a whole mug of beer down.

"Come on, Meera! I would not have come out with a bad company, definitely. It is no favor that I am doing."

Sanjay was the company that I needed to rekindle life. I wish I had gone out with him a lot earlier and oftener. I had almost walked up to Sri and Charu to ask them out, but at the very last moment, had retraced my steps back to my cubicle. There, after a long bit of hesitation, I had pinged Sanjay on the messenger. His reply was instantaneous and gratifying. "*Do you even have to ask? Let's go.*" A few minutes later, Sanjay had texted me, "*Where are you? I am in the parking lot. Don't take your car. I will drop you back to the office"*. I was drinking after a long time. I had promised to myself that I would give up on smoking and I was determined to keep it at all costs.

"Can I borrow a smoke, Sanjay?"

"Let us not light two. I am trying to cut down. We will share." He smiled as he passed the cigarette.

Guys seem to get this…glazed look in their eyes after a couple of drinks that a lot of girls, also under the spell of the same liquid, find hard to resist. I have had my fair share of 'glazy-eyed' admirers. I have also witnessed pairs who would walk into bars maintaining a careful arm's length distance between them, but who would then end up kissing or making out on the same table or in the smoking zone. It would take a crowbar to pry them apart! I am always prepared to show my middle finger to men who dared to try such tricks on me.

Sanjay's message had got me wondering if he belonged to that group of tricky men. But his behavior remained as friendly as it was in the office even after he had downed a copious amount of alcohol. The rapidly swelling crowds at Dido did not seem to be affecting him at all. He even offered a lady his seat. Soon, we were pushed to the bar stools, where I managed to find a seat. Sanjay didn't seem to mind the fact that he would have to be standing all the while. I could not help but compare him to Vineet. Sanjay was a chivalrous man, unlike that chauvinist! He was sensitive and knew exactly how to behave with a girl, all the while maintaining a respectful distance. Wow!

"How long have you been married?" I wasn't sure why I picked that particular topic. I guess I just didn't want to talk about work.

"Five years."

"Love marriage?" I asked.

"Yeah! We knew each other from junior college." He was

looking down and smiling away. See! That was exactly how I wanted to feel – happy. Every time I thought about the man in my life, I wanted to feel exactly the same way. The excitement should never die!

"Nice! Is she working?" I took another cigarette.

"No, she quit work three months after we got married. She was pregnant then. We have a son, Ishaan." Sanjay sounded happy.

I never knew all this while that Sanjay had a son. We spent a long time talking about Ishaan. Sanjay was a proud papa and the excitement was evident in his eyes every time he spoke about the little things his son did.

While the evening was so much fun, I decided to message Vineet to let him know, "*I have a meeting. I will be late*". The reply was a quick "*K*".

Ideally, I should have been irritated seeing the indifferent '*K*'. But, the evening had made me cheerful after a very long time and I forgave Vineet for that thoughtless message of his. He did not seem worried about me. He did not even check to know how I was planning to drive back home so late. In stark contrast was Sanjay's attitude. "Meera, leave your car in the office. I will drop you home. It is very late." What a gentleman!

"No Sanjay! I am a big girl. I can take care of myself. Just drop me to the office."

"Girlie! It is pointless talking to you. Hop in. I am not taking you to the office." Sanjay took me to his car.

We laughed. We sang. We talked. We ate. An evening of fun and frolic was coming to an end.

I noticed the night security guard of our apartment waiting eagerly outside the gates. I had never ever seen him getting up from his chair when I drove home after work every evening. And tonight, of all nights, the idiot was standing outside the gate like an over eager teen on his first date. And why not! Why would he let go of an opportunity to gossip about the 'loose ways' of the 'high society women' with his cronies the next day!

"Sanjay, stop the car here, please." I got out.

"Would your husband mind if he sees me with you?" he asked.

I did not even care about that. I was more bothered about the security guy than about Vineet. I was completely out!

"Naah. He won't." I waved to him and tried to walk as steadily as I could. I took two steps, but then I came back in reverse. "Do I look drunk?"

"Haha. I think you do, but it is ok. Tell him that your friends forced you to have a pint with them. I hope he doesn't mind." Sanjay drove off.

Again, I didn't care about what Vineet thinks. It was Rangaswamy that I cared about. I smiled at Sanjay again and walked towards the most important man in my life at that moment! I was looking at him with a gaze the nitwit might have mistaken for lust...but all I was really trying to do was to walk steadily.

"Good evening, madam." Ah! He even salutes me with all humility! I dislike people who put on unwanted loads of fake politeness when there is no conceivable need. Right then, that rat Rangaswamy was the very epitome of fake politeness.

"Good evening. Is sir home?" I asked.

"No madam. I thought both of you were together and must be getting late. See! I have not even switched of the lights in the parking lot. The corridor lights are on as well. Do you want me to check for him somewhere?"

Now, that was unwanted humility in the superlative! All I had asked him was a simple question but his answers were so...so elaborate. Bakshi would have loved to have him in his team!

"No, thank you." I texted Vineet as I walked in to the house. He acted as if he was unconcerned about me, but I could not treat him the same way. After all, we lived under the same roof. I had to enquire. He replied, saying that he would be home in thirty.

I was cherishing those glorious minutes even as my phone beeped "*I reached.*"

I stared at the message for a good long minute and then replied with a "*K*"

Sanjay – "*I had a great time*"

Me – "*Me too☺*"

Sanjay – "*We should go out more often. You are great company. I wonder how you managed to look that way even after five mugs down.*"

Me – "*The mallu brahmin is blessed with a lot of such skills. It shall be revealed to you…all in good time! … and yeah, we should go out more often. Sanjay, you have a beautiful son…and you are a great father…..*"

DAY OUT WITH SANJAY

Sanjay – "*I am a good friend, too. Meera, I am not sure if I should be telling you this, but for the last two months it has not been great seeing you so disturbed! That is why I jumped at the invitation last evening. Is it the marriage? I noticed that you do not talk to Sri or Charu like before. I can be your stress buster. Pour your unhappy stories out to me. Sorry I went off to sleep last night, half way through the messaging.*"

Me – "*That's okay. I slept off early too. I will see you at work soon.*"

Next day, I was feeling sprightly and bright when I stepped out of my house. Vineet offered to drop me to the office. Though I was a little surprised at his gesture, I accepted his offer. We managed to carry on a sane conversation in the car. He asked me about the meeting the previous evening and I cooked up a convincing story about our chairman being in town. As I stepped out of the car, I frantically checked my mobile to see if Sanjay had messaged. Was I in for a surprise, or what!

Sanjay – "*Where are you? I just came in and was hoping to see you here already.*"

I was smiling away and could have walked into the pool while I was busy texting. I was half way through the message "*I am a minute away. I was…*", when Vineet called.

"Hey, I was planning to take a half-day leave. Can you take one as well? Maybe, we could go out?" Vineet asked.

"Oh! I think I may not be able to. I told you that my chairman was here." Now I know why chairmen are so important to companies! They provide the perfect decoy if you are planning to do something that you don't want your husband to know!

"Alright! No problem!" Vineet hung up on me without even a 'bye'. I was not expecting much, anyway. I knew his definition of chivalry by then.

Me - *I am a minute away. I was hoping that you'd be there waiting for me as well. Looks like I'm the one who got lucky.*

Sanjay - ☺

As I entered the floor, I was overcome by a rather odd sensation. I could not bring myself to look at Sanjay, nor could I look away from him. On the occasions that I stole a glance at him, I saw that he was looking back at me as well. Had he been looking at me all this while? The odd sensation only grew odder at the team meeting. Sanjay had a slight smile as he addressed the team, prompting 'little miss smart ass' to comment, "Looks like someone's had a good night or a wonderful morning!" I could not believe my ears. How could someone so junior be cocky enough to make such a comment about a team leader? And why was the team leader himself smiling away along with the others?

Sanjay – "*So, will you tell me? What is the problem? What has been upsetting you for the last two months? We can meet and talk at the cafeteria if you want to.*"

Sanjay was not going to give up so easily.

Me – "*Don't ask me that Sanjay. I would love to continue chatting with you, but please don't ask me that question.*"

Sanjay – "*Okay. I'll not ask you again. So you must be going out for lunch with Sri and Charu, right? I will see you after lunch.*"

Me – "*Yeah. I'll see you later.*"

We continued texting right through the boring lunch and depressing conversations. Sri and Charu were very curious to know whom I was messaging. I realized that a simple 'someone' would not be enough to throw them off the scent. They kept trying to take peeks at the phone to find out who the mystery man was. So I said Vineet and that seemed to ease their curiosity a bit. I realized that Vineet could be as curious as Sri and Charu and so, to Vineet, Sanjay became 'Sandhya', a new colleague and to my curious friends, she became 'my cousin', on my phone.

Sanjay – *"There is a new place called 'Hot café' down the road from our office."*

Me – *"Nice. So are you going out for a coffee? With whom, if I may ask?"*

Sanjay – *"Well, I was planning to invite a special friend. But, not sure if she has made other plans."*

Me – *"Okay. The best way to find out is to ask her."*

Sanjay – *"What do you think? Will she say a yes or a no?"*

Me – *"Hmmm. Depends. How close is she to you?"*

Sanjay – *"Close enough to say a yes, if I ask her."*

Me – *"Then ask her☺"*

Sanjay – *"Will you….. come out with me?"*

Me – *"Yes!"*

Oh God! Was it really me who had messaged all that! What was wrong with me? The 'bad' me was turning worse! But I couldn't care less. I was finally happy. I deserved these small doses of happiness from time to time. Sanjay and I started to go out more often. We were getting good at planning this out. Sanjay would wait for me in his car a little away from office. I would leave exactly twenty minutes after he did. We pretended to the world that we were going our separate ways. Once, I even cancelled the dinner plan that Sri and Charu had initiated to re-build our drifting friendship. I did not feel guilty about it. The duo was entirely responsible for my drifting away from the group. Had they not been so eager to advise me at the drop of a hat and, instead, had listened to me while I bitched about Vineet, I would have been going out with them, rather than with Sanjay.

It was easy to manage calls and messages at home because, after all, it was only 'Sandhya'.

Sanjay – *"Hey, Bakshi is hitting the floor to announce the offsite party."*

"Guys, Guys, Guys. How is my team doing? Good results are back again. All of you are responsible for it. And…"

Me – *"Hey, that reminds me! This is the fourth quarter and I have achieved my targets. So boss, are you giving me that promotion that you promised or not?"*

"…And we have decided to celebrate it this time. We are going out on an offsite tour. As per all your requests, this time it is not going to be in Bangalore." Bakshi seemed more thrilled announcing the news than the people applauding it. He made it seem like he had crossed seven mountains, six rivers and five cities to bring us that grand prize! The team resumed work even as Bakshi, all puffed up with self-importance, continued gloating over the offsite tour.

Sanjay – *"You have special news, meerkat!"*

Me – *"Really? I can't wait for surprises. You have to tell me. NOW."*

Sanjay –*"Patience, my girl…Patience is a Virtue."*

It seemed like Sanjay was turning cuter by the day. We had become the best of friends. We knew practically everything about each other by then. The relief that I felt on having found a friend like him was too great to be described in words! It was only after I found him that I realized how suppressed my soul had felt! The relief pouring over my heart seemed to have entirely unexpected but positive effects in other aspects of my life, too. I was fighting lesser and lesser with Vineet. We still did not talk much, but we could definitely bear each other a lot better.

"How long is the trip?" Vineet asked.

"A day long. We will return tomorrow. I will be home by the

afternoon." Vineet offered to close the suitcase that I had been struggling with.

"How are you going?" Vineet was curious.

"By bus." I picked the suitcase and kept insisting that he needn't bother dropping me off at the office. Vineet had a day off and it wouldn't really have been a bother, but then I had Sanjay waiting for me just outside the gates of our building.

Taking great care to ensure that I would not be spotted by either Vineet or Rangaswamy, I got into Sanjay's car. We had also cooked up a good plan to ensure that we would be driving in Sanjay's car all the way to the site. Sanjay and I approached Bakshi separately and informed him that we would be coming on our own, rather than travel by bus with the rest of the team. While Sanjay was supposedly driving alone, I would be getting dropped by my husband who was apparently visiting an aunt who conveniently happened to be living in Chikmaglur. Also, by a happy quirk of fate, my married friends were not joining us for the offsite visit. Sri and Charu wanted to spend 'quality time' with their spouses. This ruled out the possibility of snoopy Vineet calling them to check on me.

The slight breeze and the light drizzle made our journey very pleasant. Like always, we talked, sang and occasionally stopped for *chai*. We spoke all the way. Sanjay did not disturb me when I occasionally drifted off to sleep. He kept telling me that I was worse than a kid because I would sleep off in the middle of a conversation.

We reached the resort much before the others. I went ahead to check my name on the list and I was shocked to see who I would be rooming with. It was that 'smart comments dwarf'! Why did things have to go wrong and spoil what had otherwise been such a perfect day? Darn!

"Sanjay, are you responsible for this?" I turned to him.

"No Meers, but Bakshi did ask me about the two of you and I

happened to tell him that you are not exactly the best of friends."

What! I looked at Sanjay in exasperation. He pretended not to notice and walked away sipping his coke. But then he was simply too cute to stay angry with for long. I decided that the 'smart comments dwarf' was not worth sparing a thought for. After all, I would only have to put up with her when it was time to retire for the night. Sanjay and I went out to explore the town. He spoke fluent Kannada with the local people. I had never heard him conversing in that language. It was way too impressive for a Delhi-bred guy, who had only been three years in Bangalore.

I returned alone to the resort after our brief exploration. Bakshi was in the lobby, directing people to their rooms and shouting instructions on maintaining decorum. The irritating dwarf was the only one to notice Sanjay's absence. "Meera, where is Sanjay?" I wanted to say something that would have made ears turn red in embarrassment. But, I settled for a more civil, "How would I know? Call him."

Sanjay walked in a while later and made his way straight to where Bakshi was standing. After he greeted the team, he winked at me when no one was looking.

I found that I could not bear to put up with the rest of the team at the resort. While Sanjay was busy talking to the management team, I had my cheap thrills watching him check my messages amidst all the serious talks. He would initially jerk when the phone vibrated. I was totally amused by the confused expression on his face every time he read my message.

Me – *"I hate it here. Can we not do anything that is close to fun?"*

Sanjay – *"What is on your mind? Wink wink."*

Me – *"You have a dirty mind. Don't even think about it!"*

Sanjay – *"Do you want to leave the resort? We can drive all night... stop by for occasional chais and go home in the morning. What say?"*

Me – *"Are you sure that Bakshi is going to be fine? What do we tell him?"*

Sanjay – "*I will tell him that I am dropping you somewhere close by, where your husband is going to pick you up. I will come back is what I will tell him. He is not even going to notice if I don't come back at all.*"

I almost jumped with joy! Summoning all my acting skills, I told the team how disappointed I was that I would not be able to spend time with them! Soon, we were out of the resort. I gave Sanjay a friendly hug for the great plan he had hatched. We drove off. Initially, we drove through all the deserted roads around the place. We stopped at a handicrafts store to buy something for Sanjay's little one. It was tiring for Sanjay to drive continuously and he wouldn't trust me with the wheels. So we decided to park our car at a Coffee day outlet on the highway. The guards allowed us to park the car inside. We ordered the nth *chai* for the day.

"Meera, I want to know about Vineet and you. Sorry, I asked you again but I am as curious as a girl, now. I want to know about him."

Out of the blue, Sanjay had sprung this question on me. Maybe he had this question in his mind all the time. I was not prepared to answer and I didn't want to answer. But…

"My husband and I are struggling through life, Sanjay. We are like strangers living under the same roof!"

The look on Sanjay's face revealed that he had been expecting this answer. I talked to Sanjay about Steve, Vineet and how my parents arranged this marriage for me. He seemed to understand me more than anyone else. He sat through my outpourings of grief patiently, until I could discuss my woes no longer. Even spending a night in company of the dwarf seemed a better prospect in comparison!

Sanjay sat there quietly watching me grow distressed. He seemed to have made up his mind to stay in the parking lot a while longer. We bribed the guards and paid them to get us some books. We even gave the guards a bottle of Vodka and some money for having allowed us to stay on in the lot. I was tired of the songs being played, but didn't have the strength to reach out and change them. I looked out of the window, as a gentle drizzle trickled down the glass pane. I could not remember the last time I had enjoyed the rains so much, but then I realized that it was the Vodka beginning to take effect.

"Meera, what if both of us were unmarried?"

I froze, not sure if I was supposed to answer that question.

Sanjay answered, instead. "We would be getting married right now. I am not sure as to why I am feeling this way. But, if I had an option, I would be driving straight to a place that would allow us to be together for the rest of our lives."

I could live in that moment forever! I had been subconsciously fighting my heart all this while, refusing to believe that I was falling for Sanjay. But now the mystery was solved. I was in love with Sanjay. The feelings were mutual. I was so ready to get married to him right then. I had imagined being with someone like Sanjay. But, at that moment, I realized that that 'someone' could be Sanjay himself. My hands were trembling with fear…or love. I just could not be sure.

"I love you, Sanjay."

"I love you too, sweetheart." He grabbed me and kissed me.

We could not stay off each other the entire night. We had our hands locked all the while. We were not talking anymore. We just let the songs play, without bothering that the list was looping endlessly. I watched him sleep. He never let go of my hand.

I knew that he had meant every word that he said and that he loved me more than anything else. I knew that we had an uphill struggle ahead. I would have to talk to Vineet. Sanjay would have to talk to his wife. I would love to have his son with me. But, things aren't that easy. We'd have to figure it all out. With all my love, I kissed his hand. "Good night, sweetheart." I slept, with my head resting on his shoulders. I felt him snuggling up to me.

NO MORE... VINEET

"How was the party?" Vineet asked, almost as soon as I had stepped into the house.

"Good."

"How come you are back so early?" Vineet's questions were never ending.

"I did not feel like staying. Sanjay wanted to leave early and I just tagged along." I emphasized the Sanjay bit a little, hoping to initiate the conversation that had been playing on my mind all the way back. But Vineet seemed least bothered. In fact, he even offered to make me a cup of coffee. How on earth was I going to tell him!

Me - "*Baby, did you reach? Lots of kisses.*"

"Your mother called me when she couldn't reach you. You should call her back. I told her about your offsite visit. She was surprised that you never told them."

"I will talk to her." My eyes were fixed on the phone. I was missing Sanjay already. I wanted to meet him, talk to him. My heart was beating hard. Somewhere, in my head, I could hear him calling my name "Meera...Meera". Then I felt a hand on my shoulder and I started involuntarily. It was Vineet and he had a mug of coffee in his hand. "Meera...you are looking so lost! I called out to you so many times! Just wanted to ask how much sugar you'd like in your coffee."

"One spoon, please." A message beeped on my phone. "*I reached, too.*"

"*Tired? Go to sleep.*" I had not really meant that! But it looked like Sanjay had taken me at my word and actually gone to sleep! He hardly messaged me all day. I spoke to *amma*, who was understandably upset that I was not calling them more often. She wanted me to come home as it was a Sunday, but I was in no mood at all. To top it all, Vineet's friend Reshma decided to pay us a visit. I was simply in no mood to play the gracious host either.

I got invited to lunch with the 'mad gang'. I had made the mistake of accepting that invitation once before! It had been as disastrous a lunch as I could ever remember. We had gone to this restaurant where an EPL match was being shown on a large screen TV. Vineet's gang was rooting for the universal favorite, Man-U. I got a firsthand feel of their passion for football and Man-U when the guys jumped off their seats and swore at the Sunderland forwards, every time they made their way towards the United goal.

I stood my ground in the face of a determined effort by both Vineet and Reshma to coax me to join them for lunch. Ultimately, I prevailed and they went out, giving me the space I so craved. I was missing Sanjay. Badly! I could understand his need to be with his son, but the thought of him with his wife was unbearable! I wanted to grab his attention and the only means I had to do so was to text. "*Baby, did you eat something?*"…"*What are you doing?*"…"*Missing you loads, love*".

Sanjay did not ping me for a long time. Had he confessed to his wife about us? Or, perhaps, he had just been sleeping after the long drive? After all, he had driven for about sixteen to seventeen hours at a stretch! He deserved all the rest he could get. "*Hey Meera, I am tired. Can we talk tomorrow?*" I did not mind at all. I was happy to just keep looking at the message several times that day. As a rule, I kept my phone inbox clean by deleting old messages. But in Sanjay's case, I had made an exception and saved thirty-five messages! They weren't exactly declarations of love or anything, but I didn't really care. All that mattered was that they were messages from the man I loved. "*Take care, baby☺.*"

Unlike most Mondays, when I used to drag my feet to work, I found myself eagerly awaiting the Monday following the offsite trip weekend. This was to be the first 'official' day of our relationship! I drove to work as fast as I could. This time, I was keen to make it to office before Sanjay did. I wanted to feel the thrill and pain of waiting. While the entire team had been chilling over the weekend, our clients seemed to have been working overtime! How else could one explain the amount of work that had piled up! But, my heart was elsewhere. I was dying to see Sanjay. Five times the door flung open, five times I looked at it with eager eyes and five times I was disappointed!

He came at last! I had worn a pink *kurta* that he had once complimented me on. As he entered, I dropped all my work and peeped through the gap between my computer and a helmet placed on the bay across my cubicle, hoping to catch his eye.

He did not look at me. I tried a few more times, but he did not look at me even once. I knew then that something had gone terribly wrong at his place. "*Are you alright? What happened?*" I saw Sanjay check my message and then put his phone back into his pocket. I was beginning to panic. What had happened at his place! I called him, but he didn't pick the phone. Finally, in desperation, I walked up to his cubicle. Before I could say something, he cut me by saying, "Meera, you have a target of four million. Please discuss it with your team and let me know."

I stood there, as if struck by lightning! Was this a deliberate attempt to ignore me? Did our time in Chikmaglur mean nothing at all? My time in hell was far from over. Sanjay walked past my cubicle several times completely ignoring me. He even talked to that dwarf, but not once to me. I was terribly hurt, but swallowed my pride and texted him asking if he would care to join me for lunch. All I got for my efforts was a curt, "*I am busy*."

I gave up. I decided not to message him any further. He did not deserve the attention that I was giving him! I focused on work, instead. I was soon calling up all my clients and working hard to break through all those leads that had proven difficult to close. Then, it was my turn to give him the cold shoulder and walk past to meet Sri and Charu, who were in the cubicle adjacent to his. I was so thrilled to see my friends and soon we were talking and laughing happily. They asked me about the trip. "It was great, except for a few jerks who have no clue how to behave when drunk. You know, how it is!" Did that disgusting chameleon think I would cry and beg him to come back? Had he thought that I cared?

He had thought absolutely right! After I reached home, I could not stop crying. I latched the door so that Vineet would not be able to open it and walk in on me in my miserable state. I cursed myself and Sanjay. How stupid had I been to drive off with a married man in his car? He had used me! I messaged him, "*Filthy Bastard! You are the dirtiest creep I have ever met!*" No reply. "*I pity your wife, who is unaware what a creep she is sleeping with!*" No reply. "*You jerk! You thought that you could use me? I will show you what it is to mess with me!*" I was not sure as to how I was planning to teach him a lesson, but the sole purpose of the message was to vent my frustration out. No reply. I could not sleep. That Monday was indeed not like any other. It was by far the worst!

The next day, I reached office much before Sanjay. I did not look at him as he entered. But I was hoping that he would look at me. He did not. Instead, he called out the office boy for a cup of coffee and got busy. I was angry…very angry. How could he be so unaffected by my emotions! I wanted to scream at him in front of the entire office.

Me - "*I am sorry about those messages last night, Sanjay. I was so upset. What do you think I could have done? I am feeling low, Sanjay. Talk to me, please.*" All the self-righteous dignity that I had so painstakingly built up through the night came crashing down like a house on fire! I should have been ashamed of myself to be imploring to that coward, but I was a mess!

Sanjay - "*It is ok, Meera. I understand.*"

That was his reply for having behaved like a jerk! I was not going to take that.

Me - "*Sanjay, can we please talk. I will wait for you at the cafeteria.*"

Sanjay - "*No Meera, I am not meeting you anywhere.*"

Me - "*I will wait for you.*"

I waited for over half an hour, all the while trying to call and message him. He ignored it all. Finally, I was ready to explode. I marched to the elevator, determined to go down and put up a spectacle for the entire office to see! I did not care if the juniors were going to be intimidated. I did not care if Bakshi was going to throw me out of the office. As I stepped out of the elevator, I almost ran into Sanjay. One look at my face was enough to tell him that he was in deep trouble. Quickly, he persuaded me to step back into the elevator with him and we made it back to the cafeteria. He could not meet my eyes. How could he? He was guilty as hell!

"Will you open your mouth and say something?" I was furious.

"Meera, I am sorry about everything. I was high. And we had grown quite close, which is why I behaved the way I did in the car. The next day, when I got home, I realized what a mistake that had been! I have a son, Meera. Please try and understand. This will not work." He did not once look at me.

"I was drunk as well. But I did not change my mind the next day. How could you use me, Sanjay? Just because you are married does that mean you can hurt me?"

"I'm sorry, Meera, but I don't want to give you any hope. That is why I did not reply to your messages at all. I'm really sorry."

"Your silence did not help me at all, Sanjay. I am married as well but I was ready to walk out of my marriage because I thought you loved me. How miserably wrong I was!" I fumed.

"Meera, don't compare my marriage with yours. You don't like your husband. I am happily married."

I sprung out of my chair in a fit of rage, pointed a quivering finger at the miserable worm and… "Don't…don't you dare talk about my marriage…or my husband. He is not one bit like you. You are the dirtiest bastard that I have ever come across!"

I stormed out of the cafeteria, not caring to notice that the high-voltage drama had been enacted in front of some of my colleagues. I swore never to talk to him ever. I swore never to talk to any man in the office again. They were all the same! Sanjay did not bother to check even once if I was all right. He did not care about the argument or me, anymore. He was back to work in no time!

The next few days were a revelation to me. I secretly kept an eye on Sanjay. I noticed how he spoke only to those people who were of use to him or important for some selfish purpose. I noticed how he turned into this tail-wagging dog whenever Bakshi was around and how he never missed an opportunity to flatter the man. I thought of all the times when he had vented his hatred for Bakshi during our drinking sessions at Dido. And now there he was, shamelessly licking his boss' ass for whatever it was worth. I was disgusted with myself for having fallen in love with a lying cheapskate!

Days passed, but Sanjay remained unmoved. I spent those days stumbling blindly through an increasingly dark state of depression. My sleepless nights only earned me more depression and ill health. I was a wreck! I started frequenting Dido on my own. I would get drunk and then message that asshole, pleading him to come back. When the alcohol wore off, I would berate myself for sinking so low as to send the creep those messages. I had begun to realize that I needed to move on and that there wasn't the remotest chance that Sanjay would change.

Date – 13 March, 2011

Dear Meera,

Inside Sales Account Manager – IA2

Congratulations, Meera. Based on your performance and your manager's assessment, we are pleased to promote you to the level of Inside Sales Account Manager – IA3.

This is just a letter of confirmation. Your revised salary and the annexure should be collected from the HR department.

We are confident that you will continue fulfilling your responsibilities effectively.

Best Regards

Anup Krishna

HR-Manager

I wanted to tear the letter to bits in front of my colleagues, who were busy celebrating the change of profiles that they had been rewarded with. As I walked past the wretched worm's cubicle to Bakshi's cabin, I couldn't help thinking that ideally I should have been talking to him about my concerns.

I asked Bakshi. "Sir, you promised me a promotion. I have achieved my targets for all those quarters that you wanted me to. Then, why am I being given just a grade level promotion?"

"Meera, talk to Sanjay." It was clear that Bakshi was not too busy to talk to me. He merely wanted to pass the question to Sanjay and wash his hands of the affair.

"Sir, you were the one who promised me. I want to hear this from you." I

"I don't have time to waste. We were considering you for a team leader's role when you had met your targets, but Sanjay and I assessed your candidature again for the role and thought that you have not done enough to deserve it. Meera, your impulsive nature and your indifference towards work is not appreciated. It was Sanjay who raised these points and I agree with him!" He raised his eyebrows like he did when he thought he had made a point that would clinch the argument. What happened to all those promises made to me in good times? How convenient was it to ignore all the hard work that I had put in?

Oh, how I wished I could reveal the true colors of his blue-eyed boy! The eyebrows that were still in the raised state like the arc of a suspension bridge, would have come crashing down . Actually, I was not sure about that. Bakshi was as much a slime ball as Sanjay.

I walked to Sanjay's cubicle. For a moment, I stood there in a dazed state. That moment, that one moment, caused the anger I felt towards him to evaporate. It was inexplicable, but I just felt totally drained of all emotions. I walked away from that place. I decided that I was never going to talk to anyone else about my misery. I had to fight this alone. I could not let it affect me anymore. I continued with my work, refusing to react to anything at all. I realized that the way I had reacted to things in the past had simply harmed me all the time, without really changing the situations that had evoked those reactions. I knew that no one in the team or the floor had any kind of respect for me, anymore. I knew deep inside that I wanted to earn that respect back. At the same time, I could not stay in a place where people were insensitive to human emotions…people who could return to their normal lives at the switch of a button, without the slightest regard for someone who was walking through hell because of them…

Dear Mr. Bakshi,

Sorry if this comes at a short notice. I would like to let you know that I will not be able to continue with my responsibilities at work due to personal reasons.

I thank you for your support. Please do relieve me at the earliest.
Regards
Meera M. Vineet

I marked a copy of the email to Sanjay as well. I wound up all that I had to do and walked out of the office with no qualms whatsoever and absolutely no regrets. I drove my car in silence… no music…no calls. I pulled into the porch and walked to my house.

As I opened the door, I was greeted by a rather unexpected sight. My parents, Nikki, Amit, the children, Vineet's parents, Vineet and Vittal *acha* were all there in the living room. "Hi Meera, it has been so long. Where have you been, bum? You don't call me like before. I see that your marriage is working wonders for you! You don't remember to call your sister, even." Nikki smiled mysteriously, sounding very happy for me.

She turned to Vineet, "I hope my sister has been a good wife to you, Vineet."

Vineet's father answered instead. "She is a lovely daughter to us. Madhav, you must be very lucky to have a daughter like Meera." He had spoken highly of someone who did not deserve even a bit of it. I was on the verge of a breakdown, so I excused myself and disappeared to the bathroom. As I stood there with my back resting against a wall, a wave of disgust swept over me. I had ruined the good life that had been handed to me by fate! I could not face anyone in that room. I had let everyone down.

Vineet and I were not a pair! But did that give me the license to invite another man into my life? What had I been thinking when I walked down that path! Had I been thinking at all!

I had kissed another man! I turned the tap on and splashed water over my face…over and over again. Was I attempting to cleanse myself? Was I attempting to rediscover the old Meera, daddy's favorite little girl? Was I still that? Over the years, I had drifted away from dad. Why did I drive away all the people who loved me? I stood there, numb, unsure what to do. Should I not be going out and thanking Vineet's father with all my heart for trusting and loving me so much? Should I not be going out and throwing myself into *acha*'s arms and crying my heart out, telling him that his daughter had sinned?

The entire family had gathered to usher in Vineet's birthday. At twelve sharp, Nikki rolled in the cake and the celebrations began. All the while, I stayed disconnected and watched on in silence. How happy everyone was! I looked at *amma* and Nikki and wondered how they managed to play the multiple roles of daughter, wife, friend and mother so effortlessly. Even with all the responsibilities, they were these two happy souls who had never complained about anything and managed to keep their lives free of all complications. I, on the other hand, had failed miserably in every role I had ever taken on in life!

14 March, 12:30 AM

Everyone had left. I pottered around, cleaning the house. Was it another self-cleansing attempt?

1:15 AM

I watched Vineet, sound asleep. Another happy soul with no worries in his simple life! I had always known that Vineet was not right for me. But what I should have known is that I was the one who was not right for anyone.

2:30 AM

I couldn't sleep. It was the guilt. I was tired of crying. I wanted to wake Vineet up and confess all that had happened. I just didn't have the guts to do so. Had I really been in love with Sanjay!

3:45 AM

My life had been one unending saga of bad decisions! I

had never understood the meaning of love. With Steve, it was infatuation. I liked spending time with him and I concluded that my feeling for him was actually love. Daddy had been more important to me. I loved him more, which is why my infatuation for Steve had eventually worn off. But I had walked off from that relationship and hurt Steve. The guilt in me had made me think of him often, even after we had broken up. That explained all my attempts at calling and messaging him. I had been a fool to mistake all that as love, though!

With Sanjay, it had been a feeling of 'life-reloaded'. I had just been happy to have someone to talk to. How I wished I had not had those text exchanges with him! I had crossed my line. *Acha* and *amma* would be devastated were they ever to know that their daughter had been in an extramarital affair. It was inexplicable why I had been behaving in such an eccentric fashion. Drinking, smoking, a secret affair – what had my life turned into!

5:50 AM

Thinking of Sanjay made me hate Meera more. My life had been ruined! Coming back to life would not be that easy. I had let everyone, including myself, down. I lay there contemplating suicide as a way to end my misery. It would have been a fairly easy thing to pop a few pills, but the thought of not being around to watch Manu and Paru growing up was too much to handle.

I had cheated Vineet and his family. How could I continue to be part of such a good family! They deserved nothing but honesty and trust.

I wished that I had never gone out with Sanjay. I wished that I had never met him. I wished that I had never joined Nexter. I wished … God! Why was my life such a mess?

6:30 AM

I wished that I had never been married!!

7:45 AM

"Hey! What's wrong? You look unwell," Vineet asked.

"Happy Birthday, Vineet"

"Thank you, Meera. But you tell me what happened. Didn't you sleep the entire night?"

"Vineet, there is something that I have been wanting to tell you." I looked away from him.

"Tell me?"

"I am sorry…but can we get separated. No. It is not you. It is me. Don't ask me anything. I don't feel happy here." I said.

Vineet continued sitting on the bed for an entire minute… then he walked away from me. I followed him to explain things. But it looked like there was no need for it. Vineet walked into the kitchen and started making coffee. I realized that the separation was as important to him as well. The feeling was mutual.

It was all for the good. There was no other way the story of Mr. & Mrs. Vineet could have ended.

PUTTING MY LIFE BACK TOGETHER

"*Amma*, ask Mangala not to clean the computer room. The cables...there is a loose connection. Ask her not to disturb it, please."

Months had passed since that day when I had announced my desire to separate from Vineet. I was at my new work place, now. I had taken time after Nexter to gather the fragments of my life and try to piece them together. Life had given me another chance to prove my worth...a chance for which I was eternally grateful. My only wish, then, was to live the rest of my life as the daughter my parents had always yearned for. I realized that every day, for the last eight months, I was being constantly put to a test called 'life'. I had been faring badly for a long time, but things were taking a turn for the better. For the first time I wanted to make a conscious effort to erase all the accumulated negativity and seek lasting peace.

Walking out of the marriage had not been easy. First, I had to face two sets of parents. And then there was Vittal *acha*, Nikki and my friends. On the one hand, I had to battle my own devils, and on the other, I had to remain strong to help my parents tide over the storm and understand that their daughter was going to be ok.

The memories of the morning that I walked out on Vineet are still etched clearly in my mind. He seemed to have recovered quickly from that initial disconnected reaction. He helped me load my bags into the boot and sent me on my way with wishes for a good life ahead. His mother had tried talking to me desperately, but I had avoided all calls…including those from my own folks. My heart sank as I pulled out of the porch and had one last look at my home…a place that I had unwillingly but surely become attached to.

All along the way, I fought back my tears, even as they stung my eyes. I was determined to put up a brave front for my parents, who would otherwise have been devastated.

Acha was at the gate, anxiously waiting for me. I had called *amma* earlier and let her know I was coming home, bag and baggage. I had not explained why. As I stepped out of the car, I avoided looking *acha* in the eye. "Go inside, Meera." He gently laid a reassuring hand on my head. It was then that the dam broke and the tears I had been fighting back for so long burst out. I collapsed into his arms and broke down. Deep inside my heart, without uttering a single word, I begged his forgiveness over and over and over again.

Though my parents had taken me in, it had taken a long time to get them to agree that a divorce was the only possible conclusion to it all. I willingly went through the pain knowing fully well that it would be nothing compared to the pain of leading a deceitful life. Initially, Nikki did her best to make me change my mind. But, eventually, she came around to seeing things from my perspective. I guess she must have realized that a life with Vineet was not something that I desired. She helped me tide over the tough times by spending as much time as she could with me.

After initially enquiring anxiously as to what had gone wrong, Vittal *acha* had broken off all communications with me for a long time. Clearly he had been upset with the way his daughter had behaved. Convincing him had been a monumental task. A divorce in the family was unheard of! It was something that happened to others, not to daughters of the family! *Achamma* made several attempts to talk me out of my decision. Rarely would an evening go by without her calling me to see if I had changed my mind. The poor thing kept calling me even after the divorce, just in case I had had a change of heart and wanted to reconcile.

My family turned out to be my greatest support during those dark times. I was grateful to have someone my own to fall back on during my struggle to restore a semblance of order to my tattered life.

Daddy advised me to not really worry about taking up a job for as long as it took to set my mind in order. He wanted me to take a long hiatus and then join him in his business. But I was determined to blaze my own trail and make it big. I had been meeting a lot of interesting people through some of my old friends. Everyone seemed to agree that I needed to bide my time and decide what I wanted to do next. As one of them put it, "This is your second innings. Make it big!" I was feeling a lot better. Each day of my life was like a new beginning. My thoughts, my mind was getting clearer. It was easier getting to know people and relating to them. My drab existence was taking on a whole new meaning.

My days began early. I unearthed and religiously followed the timetable that *amma* had insisted I follow much before I had left home a married woman. My hotheadedness or carelessness had made me disregard her words then. I now began to see the merits of her advice. Apart from adhering to her list, I also immersed myself in yoga, dance lessons, a library and an NGO. Anything that would keep me happy and the positive vibes flowing. But, above all, I enjoyed walking the streets of Bangalore, rediscovering the city I so loved. I walked down the busy roads and, for the first time, actually noticed all those places that I used to frequent with Sri and Charu in the past. One of the places was Dido. I was pleased to discover that that place no longer held the charm it once did!

And, Vineet and I was no longer a pair. We were divorced.

Bhaskaran Pillai, the director of Abhinaya Theater, was one person who influenced my life greatly during that period. I took a two-week workshop run by the theater and discovered with a great amount of satisfaction that I had the potential to emote. When I danced, sang or acted in the workshop, I felt the remnants of my depression draining out of my being.

At the end of a particularly satisfying session, Bhaskaran walked up to me and began with no preamble. "Hi, you will make a great actor one day."

"Thanks Bhaskaran. But I have no intentions of pursuing acting as a career. A friend of mine recommended your workshop and I came here just for the experience. It has been rewarding, to say the least. I did not ever believe I could act. Today's session has been an eye-opener for me." For a few fleeting moments during the conversation a shadow seemed to pass over my heart. Was this the beginning of another 'Sanjay episode' all over again! I knew that it was an irrational thought. The man had only been trying to help me expand my vistas. But, somehow, I could not help warning myself. That was how badly the Sanjay incident had scarred me! I started to walk away, but Bhaskaran simply fell into step beside me. We got talking about his career. Direction had been his first love, a dream that saw fulfillment at the relatively late age of forty-five. When we parted that day, I had a distinct feeling of having met a man destined for great things in life!

It was Bhaskaran who first encouraged me to tap the creative side of my being. He made me realize that I was not just meant to be a glorified sales girl. The seed of pursuing a career in fine arts started germinating in my mind. I took to meeting a lot of artists from various disciplines. Nayana Suresh, an accomplished dancer, was one among them.

Nayana had a dance academy on the outskirts of Bangalore. I

visited the school with a notepad in hand and a camera around my neck. I had not intended to, but ended up spending a long time with her and her students. She introduced me to various dance styles that I had only heard of, previously. Upon learning that I had been instructed in *Bharatnatyam* for eleven years, she insisted that I dance with her. Was dance my true calling, then?

Gradually, I met up with a lot of artists. I found that there were more than five hundred dance schools in Bangalore and an equally astonishing number of music academies, acting schools, painting classes and photography courses on offer as well. I spoke to a lot of people, recorded my interviews with them and took pictures of their schools and students.

I could sense my heart growing lighter with every passing day…as if I was getting closer to finding a purpose in life. And, then, one day, while I was sifting through all the material I had accumulated from my various meetings, I had a breathtaking revelation! For a few moments, I sat there, eyes closed, experiencing the kind of profound calmness that had eluded me all my life. I had indeed discovered a purpose in life! I would tell the world the story of these amazing people who were selflessly passing on their knowledge and ensuring that our culture would remain alive in the hearts of the generations to follow.

Mukta, the offspring of my newly enlightened soul, rolled out two months later.

Soon, I had friends helping me out with ideas on the magazine. A couple of them even joined the initiative and soon we were three partners. The three of us had a lot in common. We were all estranged from a corporate life and wanted to be involved in a project that was close to our hearts. At the same time, we also had unique skills that played a vital part in running the business. Malini Vijaykumar, an erstwhile accountant, was now handling the printers and negotiations. I, along with two freelancers, managed the content and pictures for the magazine. A particular column encouraging new talent turned out to be a big hit. We received letters by the dozens from readers and struggling artists. **Mukta** became a well-appreciated forum for such genuine talent. Soon, television channels, theater groups, and even cinema producers started approaching us in search of fresh faces.

Drishti Jain, the third partner, took the entire responsibility of the logistics, shipment and the thousand other details that went with that sort of thing. Malini and I did not have to bother about the magazine once it was printed and entrusted into Drishti's capable hands. **Mukta** was soon a subscription magazine that reached out to fifty thousand individuals within three months of its launch. I was busy enjoying my work, my passion.

"Hey Meera!"

"Heeyyy Charu! How have you been?" I was so thrilled to have heard her voice after ages, albeit on the phone. I had not confessed to anyone how badly I had been missing my two best friends! Before quitting, I had not been able to confide in them as to the actual reason for putting down my papers. So it had been a relief when Charu called that day.

We spoke for a long time. I was dying to meet Sri as well.

We agreed to meet that evening at Bristo. This coffee place had edged Dido out and now reigned as my favorite hangout.

"So that is the reason why you ignored us at work! Now it is all becoming clear. It is ok, dear. We are friends. We would never have judged you." Those were the most comforting words that my best friend Sri could have spoken to me.

"Yeah! I realized that it was a mistake and I could not have lived an extra minute with Vineet with all that pent up guilt." I confessed.

"How is Vineet? Was he okay with the divorce?" Charu asked.

"I thought so, Charu. But his father happened to tell me that he had taken it very badly. I don't think he understands Vineet very well. Vineet is fine. I heard that they are looking out for another match for him. You know what; I may actually be running into him next week. We have a feast to attend at a common family friend's house. I will be meeting him after five months! I am more worried about meeting his mother."

"Was there too much trouble between you guys? Umm…I am just being curious. Maybe I shouldn't have asked." Charu asked.

"No Charu, I will tell you. There was no love between us."

"Have you guys made out, anytime?" The Sri that I knew so very well was back! She had surprised me by that initial heavy 'friends don't judge' talk. It somehow didn't become her at all. I was far more comfortable with this familiar 'foot-in-mouth' behavior.

"Haha! Mom asked me the same questions, but she tried beating around the bush. When I obstinately refused to take her subtle hints, she, out of exasperation, asked me point blank if I had had sex with him anytime. Well, the answer is NO. We simply didn't love each other for that to happen."

"Maybe it was, Meera. Vineet is a nice guy…at least much better than Ansh. I couldn't help observing you and Vineet, when you guys were together. Do you know that he could never take his eyes off you, when you weren't looking? And I think of how Ansh used to treat me during those initial days of marriage. He just wanted a wife to showcase to the world! To him, the marriage was more like a license to have an affair with someone. Don't look so shocked, Sri. I am not making this up. Do you know, his own family has caught him several times with other women! But it doesn't seem to make a difference at all. Though he has failed as a husband, he has been a good father, guys. After Deepta was born, Ansh started spending more time at home. But then it didn't take him long to go back to his unfaithful ways. You may be wondering why I'm putting up with all this. I am not a very strong person, Meera. I need a companion to live. I am living with the hope that someday things would change for the better." Charu's voice had been choked with emotion while she had been making that shocking confession…and by the end of it, she was weeping softly. I always knew that Ansh had not been a good guy. He was a chauvinist who derived some kind of pleasure by publically criticizing and demeaning his wife. On the evening of that party at Charu's house, I had seen him pull a girl he had been eying all evening to a corner and kissing her. I had been shocked, but hadn't wanted to upset Charu. I couldn't bring myself to rock the blissful world that she had built around her family.

Sri and I held Charu's hand to comfort and assure her that her life would eventually turn out okay. We spoke for a long time and parted promising to keep in touch. I was pleased that Charu had finally unburdened herself.

I was about to leave the place when I felt a tap on my shoulder. I turned around to find myself looking into the smiling grey eyes of Steve.

"How are you, Meera?" he asked.

"Steve! What a surprise! I am good, Steve. How are you?" Wow! This day was turning out to be a blast from my past. First my friends and now Steve!

"How is your husband?" he asked. "Charu was telling me that you guys are made for each other."

"Well, I'm not so sure about that. A lot has happened, Steve. Maybe, it is better unsaid."

"No, talk to me." Steve had come with a girl. He signaled her to wait inside, along with some other friends.

I spoke to Steve about everything that had turned my life on its head since we had broken up. I told him about how the experience had made me value life, trust and honesty. Steve was very upset about the way Sanjay had treated me. He was genuinely happy to know that I had started something of my own.

"Meera, I have known you for a little while only…but that was more than enough to understand you completely. You are a very nice girl. You are just unsure about your life. Remember the last time we met here at Bristo? I realized that day that my notion about you was right. You are your father's girl, Meera. You are just like him and so are your choices. He would never have liked me…and though you liked me a lot then, the feeling would've eventually worn off once the initial excitement died down. I don't know much about Vineet, Meera, but from what I've heard from Charu, I firmly believe he is the right guy for you. But, then, that's just my gut feeling. Maybe what happened was all for the good. You take care, Meera. And keep in touch."

"Bye, Steve."

It felt so good to have met Steve. It was so reassuring to know that he did not hate me. I was also glad to have finally made up with my dearest friends. I would call them, especially Charu, more often. She would never be able to go through the mental distress of a divorce, because, unlike me, she was still in love with her husband.

I WAS MEETING VINEET...AGAIN!

That day, the question 'what would Meera be wearing to Uncle Swaminathan's puja feast?' seemed to be predominantly occupying everyone's mind. Nikki, *Amma*, and even *Acha* seemed to have opinions in that matter and had tried everything from subtle hints to outright suggestions to bring me around to their point of view.

"Wear that bottle green salwar, Meera." Nikki, as usual, had caught me off guard in my room and offered unsolicited advice on picking the right dress for the occasion.

"Meera, wear a chain. Your neck looks bare." Now, what could *amma* have been hinting at?

It didn't take me long to figure out that it was all about Vineet. Unlike me, the rest of my family had still not gotten over the separation and was still clinging to some ghost of a hope. I had to let them be. I had hurt them enough and if taking in their suggestions without argument was one way to atone for the distress I had caused, then so be it.

We drove off to uncle Swaminathan's place in my car. I stole a quick glance at my family. Seated to my left, dressed in a pristine white silk *mundu* and a matching kurta, *acha* looked nothing short of dapper. I noticed how graceful *amma* appeared in her *kancheevaram* and Nikki and her children were sure to be the stars of the show, dressed as they were in their best designer ethnic wear. I couldn't help smiling to myself, thinking of a previous visit to the same uncle's place for yet another of his frequent pujas. It seemed like the entire family had had a fashion disaster then! What a makeover this was, in comparison!

I had contemplated this puja visit several times in my mind. I had not been and was still not prepared to face Vineet's parents. I hadn't seen them for a long time. I had consented to attend the function only because daddy had badly wanted me to go. On entering the house, I tried to make myself as inconspicuous as possible by hiding behind my family. But any feeble hopes I had nurtured of getting through the evening unnoticed was dashed when I saw uncle Swaminathan make a beeline for me. My luck!

My earliest memory of this particular uncle was of a man who simply loved to talk. Even as children, Nikki and I had been forced to sit through long lectures that could suitably be titled 'the facts of life according to Mr. Swaminathan'. Eventually, various other uncles also spotted a made-to-order audience in me and took every available opportunity to talk to me about how focused in life I needed to be. After putting up with the initial few discourses, Nikki had managed to give these big mouths the slip. And she had done exactly that even on this occasion. Even as the portly frame of uncle Swaminathan approached me, with questions written all over his chubby face, I quickly glanced around to see that Nikki had conveniently disappeared. In fact, my entire family had done a Houdini and left me alone to face the barrage that was sure to come.

"Hello Meera, how are you? Did daddy force you to come? Don't worry. We all go through rough patches in life. Take it positively. What is your plan, next? I heard from your father that you have started a new company! But money is not everything. You should have a family of your own. Parents will not be able to ....."

Even as he was talking, I drifted off. My mind was set on a

more immediate issue. I had to take all necessary precautions not to bump into Vineet or his parents. After politely nodding a few times and adding a few 'u-huhs' for effect, I excused myself and escaped to the balcony on the first floor. This, I reasoned, was the safest place in the entire house and my best chance of keeping out of sight. On the flip side, however, this ensured that I was blind to the happenings downstairs. I had a tough time biding my time all alone, especially since the smell of food that was wafting in from the kitchen was irresistible. I started nursing thoughts of stepping out to grab a bite. Then, vivid pictures of *acha* cornering me that evening so long ago, when I had left the relative safety of my room in search of food came flooding to my mind and I abandoned the thought. This time I was staying put!

"Meera! How are you *ma*? I met your mother downstairs. She told me you are up here. What are you doing here all alone?"

I could not believe that it was Vineet's mother who was talking to me in so gentle a voice. I had imagined this inevitable confrontation many a time, and on all occasions, it involved an outburst of tears or a volley of curses or, at the very least, barbed questions as to why I had put their family through all the pain. I must have done something good in life to deserve all this love, I thought as I hugged her and apologized for all that had happened and most importantly for hardly having spoken to her in the months leading to and after the divorce. She was all for leading me downstairs to meet Vineet's father, an offer that I politely but firmly declined. I was simply not ready to meet him. Had I not let him down so horribly mere hours after he had praised me to the skies on Vineet's birthday! Seeing my discomfiture, Vineet's mother did not press me further. We laughed and talked for a while until her son came up looking for her.

Vineet! Was it the first time I was observing him that close! He had grown lean. He had curly hair? How come I had never noticed! He looked pale but pleased to see me, unlike what I had expected.

"Hi, how are you?" Vineet asked.

"I am good, Vineet. How have you been?"

"Good, Meera. *Ma*, papa is looking for you. Sita aunty is here." Vineet's mother excused herself, and before I could protest, rushed downstairs to go meet this aunty. Why do aunties have such hopelessly bad timing! How was I going to handle this encounter with Vineet all by mrself?

"You are looking nice, Meera." Vineet said. "Hey, I heard about the company, your work and partners. Congratulations. I always thought that the Nexter job was not for you at all. This work suits you better any day."

Now, how had Vineet come to know about my company! Then it dawned upon me that the two families were still very much in touch. Vineet knew a lot about my venture. He told me about how one of his friends was praising the magazine once and how he had quietly basked in the knowledge that he had known the founder.

I found myself warming to the subject. We spoke for a long time. It was as if a small floodgate had opened somewhere and my dammed up heart was venting it out. But, however much I tried, I just could not let him in on what had transpired between Sanjay and me. I told him about the promised promotion that never came my way and how Sanjay and Bakshi had orchestrated the whole charade. It just gave Vineet another chance to express his dislike for Sanjay, but this time I made no objections. I realized that he had perhaps been right about Sanjay all the time. No manager that cared for his team would ever call a female employee up on a Sunday, especially if she had been married recently. Had Sanjay guessed that my marriage was on the rocks? Had he been deliberately trying to take advantage of the situation and getting close to me? What a fool I had been!

Vineet continued. "I used to always wonder if a Sanjay or a Madhu were responsible for us not being together any more. But no! We were just not made for each other. I had kind of realized that right on the day we first met, but kept believing that things would eventually be fine. That day was special for me. I had just got a promotion. And, you know how things are between me and dad right? He had not spoken to me in a long while, but that day he walked into my room and asked me about my work and promotion. On the way back home from your place, he smiled at me and said that he liked you and your family very much. I could not have made him happier, Meera. You and your family were entirely responsible for that smile of his. That meant the world to me and I simply had to say yes to you."

I stood there, soaking it all in. It was a strange feeling. I realized that it was the first time ever that I was quietly listening to him talk. I felt the cobwebs that had enveloped my mind clearing and a wonderful sense of understanding beginning to dawn. I was finally learning to understand Vineet. He had not been wrong at all. Steve and Charu had been right all along. And what was more, it did seem like Vineet and I had a few things in common, starting with an intense devotion to our fathers.

"I know I never shared this story with you when we were together, Meera. I just didn't see how it was important. Perhaps, I thought, we'd talk about it in a casual moment together, but that just didn't happen. That day, Meera, you were simply the best girl in the whole world. A girl who had brought so much happiness into our lives."

It was time to reflect. Or was it really? The talk we had just had was perhaps not enough to make us reconsider the decision we had made. But I realized that we could still be friends.

Vineet said, "But, everything feels so good now. I am busy with my job. Girish and I have been travelling to see places. We have put together a bucket list and there are only a few things left to do. Well, it was Girish who edited the bucket list and so items like 'publishing my story' and 'starting a venture' have been removed. According to him, one should never overestimate one's intellectual limits."

Vineet and I had our first hearty laugh together. It was pleasant to talk to him, something that I had never realized.

"You deserve a better life, Meera. You need a man who is intelligent, smart and someone who can appreciate you. We could not even strike a decent conversation together. I know that I was responsible for it. How could I expect you to understand me all the time and act accordingly? I wish I had communicated better with you so that you could have understood me. I just didn't bother to do so. I am not angry with you at all. You deserve someone better."

Well, I got the point! He didn't have to keep driving the thought that I deserved someone better into my head! Suddenly, I did not want to talk to him anymore. The recent past had been a horrid time and there was no way I was going to get into that turmoil again. Well, what the heck, Vineet didn't want it either.

We went downstairs together. I met his father, who seemed as happy as ever to see me. After the initial awkwardness had worn off, we spoke for a short while, the conversation mainly consisting of a profusion of apologies on my part.

On the drive back home, my heart felt heavy. I had not made an attempt to know Vineet, while we were married. He was not a bad guy after all. I could relate to him. I just wished and hoped that he found happiness in his life as well. Was I making a mistake again? I could not help thinking about him. Everyone the car was quiet. Probably, everyone was ruminating on that evening with the Hariharan family. I noticed Manu happily sinking his teeth into a bar of chocolate that Vineet had given him. I remembered how Vineet used to always speak high of Manu and tell me how he would grow up into a very intelligent boy. Vineet had actually liked my family as well. Memories of Nikki and Vineet talking, singing and cooking together in the kitchen came flooding into my mind. Had I not noticed all this before? He was a nice guy. Just that we would not have been able to live together.

Now I knew why Vineet had agreed to marry me. I wished he had told me earlier. But, wait! I had not told him why I had consented to marrying him either. We had never spoken like this before. He likes to travel! I had always thought that Vineet could not think beyond his home, office and Bangalore. The picture of him that I had carried around all this while had been completely wrong. He was a sensitive guy. He was a nice guy. He was indeed a very nice guy.

As I broke from my reverie, I noticed *acha* looking at me in the rearview mirror. I guess my thoughts must have shown clearly on my face, for he smiled and gestured with his eyes that it was all going to be fine.

A DAY OF REVELATION

It is fascinating how work tends to pile up if you turn your eye away from it even for a small length of time. Unfortunately, I did not have the chance to stand and admire this phenomenon because it was my work that was in question and Uncle Swaminathan's puja was entirely to blame for thoroughly upsetting my timetable. I had a deadline to meet and was just not making any progress in that general direction. I tried to focus on the pictures, interviews and columns, but my mind kept wandering. I had never experienced such a lapse in concentration since the inception of *Mukta*. I tried all the usual, time-tested methods of realigning my mind – I walked around, did a quick breathing exercise, had a cup of tea – but to no avail. Much as I hated to admit it, I was thinking about Vineet.

When all efforts to exorcise the thoughts of Vineet from my mind failed, I did the next best thing. I succumbed to it. I let my mind wander freely to our time together and thoughts started straying randomly. The day after I first went out with Sanjay, Vineet had offered to drive me to the office. He had been talking about so many things in the car. How cheerful he had sounded! He had wanted to take me out and had volunteered to take leave as well, but I had shown no interest in the idea or even the conversation. He had at least tried. I remembered how he had made earnest efforts to sort things out between us over the next few days and how I had just driven him away. The thoughts just kept coming. That lunch he had invited me to with the rest of his gang that I had adamantly refused to go to. My favorite pizzas delivered at home, on the weekends I had been too bored to cook. Those mugs of steaming coffee that mysteriously surfaced when I needed them the most. Those phone bills paid without me even being aware of it. I had been so busy seeking happiness outside, when it had been right beside me all the time!

I recalled that evening when the entire family had gathered for his birthday. How happy Vineet had been when he offered me the first piece of cake! He had wanted to talk to me as well, but muddled as I was, I had walked away. I had been very unfair to him. I had never given him a chance to talk. I was busy being me. I had not listened to my own parents when they kept assuring me that Vineet was a nice guy and that he would keep me happy. I had been wrong, clearly. What if I had given our relationship a chance? Would we have been happy?

Perhaps not. Maybe I was just sympathizing with him. I was again confusing it with 'love'. It was just a feeling of sympathy. Vineet and I could not have made it far. Yeah! Darn! Why am I thinking about him? Focus, focus Meera!

"What are you doing, Meera?" *Acha* had unexpectedly walked into my room.

"*Acha*.. Nothing. I was just trying to work on the next issue, but was not able to. My mind is worked up, I guess."

"Because you met Vineet?" he asked.

"No, No, No…," I protested. "It is just that… I am not sure if I am feeling lazy. Something like that. It has got nothing to do with Vineet."

"Meera, I was watching you in the car. It is Vineet. I wanted you to meet him. Not because I was hoping you would get back together but to make you realize that your assumptions about Vineet were wrong. When you walked out on him and came home,

I realized that my daughter was making a mistake. You said things about Vineet that I could not believe. I was shattered, but then I forced myself to sit down and ponder over what could have gone wrong. It all boiled down to a total breakdown of communication between the two of you. I wanted you to realize that and know that you had grievously misjudged a good boy. But, knowing my daughter, I realized how futile it would be to force my views into her head. It would have done more harm than good."

It was true. *Acha* had hardly said much after I came back to my place. His words, as few and far-in-between as they were, were always to comfort. Today and after a very long time, the most important person in my life was helping me place things and my life itself, in better perspective.

Acha continued. "Even as a kid, you'd be provoked easily and lose your temper at the smallest things…and this would cause your mother and me a lot of distress. But we ignored it because we loved you. After you started working, it was even more difficult to control you. Whenever I tried to stop you from doing something wrong, you reacted in a way that made me fear that you would walk out of the house or do something even more drastic. I thought it wise to remain silent and watch my daughter from afar. We let you live your own life on your own terms and never interfered. My heart broke to see you making all the mistakes. Whenever I saw a packet cigarettes popping out from your bag or a bill from a bar, I would be shattered. Like many parents, I decided that a marriage was the answer to it all. But I honestly did not realize that I was interfering in your life again and that the decision I had taken, however good the intention, would wreck your life like this."

I sat there in disbelief, realizing how I had been hurting my parents all along. For the first time I saw that they had been hurt by the way I was, more than by the divorce itself.

"On Vineet's birthday, when his father told us that you were a daughter to them, I was so proud of you. You had made me rise in esteem in their eyes. All the disappointment and worries that you had ever caused me dissipated in that one second and all I wanted to do was to hold you tight and let you know that you were my sweetest daughter."

Daddy's eyes welled up when he said this and I could not fight my tears as well. I had let down my hero time and again. In that thoughtless instant when I walked out on Vineet, I had crushed the pride my father felt in me.

All my strength and resistance broke in that one instant and I fell into *acha*'s arms and cried my heart out. "*Acha*.... Sorry *acha*."

"It is okay, sweetheart. I am glad that my daughter has bounced back as a good girl. She has realized her mistakes and she is going to keep herself happy. That is all we want. It is going to keep us happy, forever."

I was determined to tell *acha* about Sanjay. I had to confess to him about the biggest mistake of my life. I could not keep it within me anymore.

"*Acha*.." I was crying bitterly. "It was an office thing. On Vineet's birthday, I was upset. I have been a bad girl, *acha*. I had gone out...."

Before I could say anything more, daddy stopped me.

"I knew that you had erred. It was your conscience that was pricking you. When you came home from Vineet's place, I knew it all. You should know, Meera, that we all make mistakes. We are not perfect. I have had my own share of mistakes. We cannot brood over it all the time. You will be forgiven when you choose to never make that mistake again. Your life is bound by a lot of people around you. A part of your life is mine, your mother's, Nikki's and the children's'. We will not be able to bear it if you remain hurt. It was not easy to watch you cry, Meera. We all cried silently in our hearts. Nikki was the most affected. She felt responsible for having pushed you to that state. She kept admitting to us that she should have supported you when you were not happy with this marriage. She may not have apologized to you, but all that she did for you after that was her way of saying how sorry she was."

The past few months had been days of revelation for me. For the first time ever I was getting to know my own people better.

"We should be very discreet when we judge anyone, Meera. There may be times when people don't behave the way we want them to. That does not mean that they are wrong. It could happen to us as well. We may have hurt others unknowingly. It is the same case when people do not react the way we want them to. They might be doing it unknowingly, as well."

The day had turned out to be a blessing. I had got to know Vineet better and daddy had made me understand that the guilt I was living in had to be flushed out of my system. I just had to make sure not to make those mistakes again.

"Life keeps throwing you these opportunities. It is up to you to grab them. Sometimes you get it right. Many times you don't. But those mistakes don't stop you from living. You should learn to rise from your mistakes, from your failures. It is never too late. You learn the hard way. People who come up in life through their mistakes and failures are blessed. Those bitter lessons in life will make you a good human being, who is sensitive to other people who are going through such difficulties."

"Don't ever give up, sweetheart! You are making us proud through your new initiative. We are very happy to have such a talented daughter. You are doing a great service to people who are struggling in life. Your father is always going to support you, come what may!"

I can't describe how I was feeling then! My daddy, my hero, my best friend was really very very special to me. I vowed to myself never to take a wrong turn in my life, again. I was determined to make him happy. I had to call Nikki and talk to her to let her know what a lovely sister she was. *Amma* had to be given a kiss, right away.

Life was giving me a second chance. I had to call Vineet up to let him know how right he was. It was he that deserved someone better. I had to tell him that.

Should I have to tell him that?

Well, he deserved someone good.

Yeah! He did.

He surely did.

VINEET WAS RIGHT... ALWAYS RIGHT!

"Meera, what happened? Is everything ok? Just send us the data and we will work on the articles." Malini had agreed to take care of my work for the time being, but I realized that this was not a long term solution. I had a premonition that trouble and tough times were lurking around the corner. Muddled as I was, I still realized that my state of mind was no excuse to shirk responsibility any longer. But, I was feeling very restless and there was no way I could do justice to Diya Abraham's article. The only option was to let Malini handle it.

I was constantly thinking about a man who had meant nothing to me just a couple of days ago. I made a conscious effort not to think about him by keeping myself busy. When I tired of mental exercises, I resorted to physical activities as a means to shut him out. But to no avail. Whenever I took a break from the exertions, my mind would gravitate towards Vineet. The desperation I felt could be sensed by the fact that I was keen to do the most mindless things, like braiding Paru's Barbie's hair, an offer I realized was long standing, to keep my mind Vineet-free. Nothing worked. Hariharan Junior had raided, conquered and happily settled down in my thoughts. I was constantly looking out for work, like that genie out of the bottle. I skipped from one task to the other, not caring to give my mind or body a break.

Working from home had other consequences as well. "Meera,

what are you up to? I am glad that you are doing all that work, but could you please save it all for another day? I have to go out tomorrow and so I can leave you to all the household work, I hope?" Though it sounded like a request, it was more an instruction. And that was the fallout of working too hard on 'official stuff', right under my mom's nose. But I wasn't going to let mom's opportunistic comments stop me. I kept going.

"*Vineet wore a blue shirt, the day he came to meet me*".

Darn! Maybe I should head to the kitchen and cook my way out of trouble. I had made rapid strides with my culinary skills of late and now it seemed like my last shot at salvation. How the mighty had fallen!

"*How the hell had that that glutton Girish stuffed all that food into his mouth! He just could not stop eating! Didn't that idiot see me glaring at him? How could he? For that, he'd have to take his eyes off the food for at least a second, wouldn't he?*"

Damn! Damn! What was wrong with me? Cooking was not helping me either. Not only was it not letting me keep my mind off Vineet, it was actually bringing pictures of his loathsome friend to my mind!

I stepped out of the kitchen, feeling famished. And needless to say, my thoughts were still tormenting me. I sat quietly on the couch, with my eyes closed. I could feel myself sinking into the same devastating depression that had left me an emotional wreck a few months ago. I felt the same pain that had made me weak and fidgety. I dreaded it. The only difference was that I was no longer able to vent it out. My tears had all drained.

The reason for all the pain this time was Vineet. Not because he had done something wrong, but because he had been right all the time! I had misjudged a man who had been my husband. I had been so self-indulgent that I had failed to acknowledge the existence of another human being in the same house, who was entirely entitled to having a completely different set of thoughts.

I relived the moments we had spent together. The day we had moved into our apartment in Chandra Nagar had been awful. I had already started nurturing thoughts of separation, while Vineet had been building hopes of a life together. Our conversations always led to a fight because I was constantly judging him. Vineet could never speak his mind freely because his frustrated wife was too far gone into a world of her own creation to care. When had I felt worse? When I got married to Vineet? Or now, when I had all the freedom in the world and was still feeling as miserable as a lout?

And what bloody right did Vineet have to be so good looking? He was looking so super cute at the Puja the other day and those bimbos could not take their eyes off him! Not that I care…Yeah, what do I care. His latest glamorous avatar was not going to make me regret my decision one bit.

I had to talk to Vineet. I had to unload my heavy heart by letting him know that I had been wrong. Should I call him? Wait, I think I should call Nikki and tell her all about it. No wait, that would be as good as telling *amma* and the rest of the clan from Palakkad to Philadelphia! Wrong move!

"Charu! I am very worried, Charu! I know that there is no point talking to him again but I can't think straight even for a minute. I am unable to work or eat or sleep or even stay calm for a second! Could this be guilt?" I had called up Charu out of sheer desperation.

"Or could it be love?" Charu teased.

"Charu, please…"

"Alright Miss Guilty," she said. "It is whatever you think it is. And, I want you to meet him today."

"Meet him?" I asked, trying to sound incredulous. "Can't I just call?"

"Stop whining, Meera…call and tell him what? Have you thought about it?"

"Yeah. I will talk to him about… about…hell, I don't know! I will figure it out."

"Meera, if I were in your place I would also have not been sure about what I should be saying to him. Meet him, girl. That's the best way and there is nothing wrong in it."

Well, I did not have much trouble accepting Charu's advice, because that was precisely what I wanted to do. I was dying to meet Vineet, but just didn't want anyone to get to know just how desperate I was!

What if Vineet refuses to meet me? No, I cannot meet him. I am NOT going to meet him.

"Hey, Meera, What a surprise?"

"Hi Vineet, what's up?" After several false starts, I had finally picked up the phone.

"Nothing much." He said. "I am at work. Are you at work too?"

"Vineet, I wanted to meet you today. Can you take some time out?"

"Is everything ok, Meera?" Vineet asked.

"Everything is absolutely fine." I replied. "I just wanted to meet you."

"I have a project to wrap up and I may get busy later in the evening. But, I can step out for lunch. Do you want to meet up?" Vineet was already busy and I could sense that.

"I hope I am not bothering you." I said. "Lunch will be good."

"Great. I will meet you at the KFC near your place. Is one'o'clock good?"

"Yeah. Sounds good. Alright. See you."

I hoped that I knew what I was getting into, because there was a spring in my step as I got ready to go. I had spent longer than usual selecting my clothes and in front of the mirror. Well, a girl has to take care of herself. Nothing unusual about that now, is there? Who the hell was I kidding!

I walked to the KFC outlet, which was just a couple of blocks away. I was glad not to be driving because in the state of mind that I was in, I would have been lucky to get away bumping into a few cars rather than running over somebody!

As I stepped into the restaurant, I received a message from Vineet saying he was five minutes away. I tried to quickly rehearse the few things that I had to tell him. I wouldn't really need much time, I figured. After all, I only had to apologize for being a mean, self-centered, illogical, egocentric, indecisive, muddled up brat who had given him grief for the best part of a year and screwed up his life for…well for the rest of his life, I guess. Now how much time was that going to take? Hell! Who could have imagined that meeting an ex would be as nerve wracking as this?

There he was, looking calm enough to send spasms of jealousy running all over me. How I wished I were in his place! Well, in all fairness, I couldn't grudge him even one bit of the serenity that he might have been feeling at that time. I prepared to face the heat. I hoped that Vineet wouldn't act indifferent. I just wouldn't be able to stand it. While I was still contemplating all these things, I saw Vineet walk in…with a bunch of familiar faces right behind!

"Hi Meera, long time. How are you?"

"I am fine. How are you, Girish? Hi Reshma, Aman. Hi Madhu!"

"She is fine. He is fine. She is fine. And so am I. And I am also famished. So let us have food." Girish had brought up the rear of the party, announced his intentions, and made straight for the counter like some heat-sensing missile. I believe he made a fleeting inquiry about my well being, but then I could never be sure. He could have been simply reading off the menu!

"Girish, remember your promise. You are going to allow Meera and Vineet have their lunch in peace. We take a different table.

Sorry Meera, that we came along. You can blame it on Vineet. We had already made plans for lunch for today before you called. You see, it happens to be Aman's last day at work and Vineet did not want to cancel the lunch plan although the rest of us would have been more than happy to postpone it." Reshma was literally pulling Girish towards another table. She had always been the caring one among the lot, but, again, I was judging them. All of them had only been nice to me.

The trouble was that the awkwardness of the entire situation had just doubled with the group landing there. But yeah, it was no fault of theirs.

Vineet led me to another table and told me that he would join me in a couple of minutes. I saw him talk to Madhu. It was only the second time I was meeting her and I thought she looked quite pretty. Vineet had spoken about her often and I had sensed that there might have been something going on between them. I had never been sure about it. In fact, the truth was that I had never actually bothered about it. My lawyer had simply forced me to put that in my divorce petition, saying that it would work in my favor. When she asked, I had just casually blurted out the slightest doubt that I had. "I don't know. I had always thought that Vineet and his colleague, Madhu were quite close to each other, but I am not sure." I regretted it many times later, especially when she brought the issue up in front of Vineet, his father and his lawyer. I sounded like one of those desperate wives who would not hesitate to stoop to any level to get out of a marriage as long as there was a good alimony in it. I had not been able to face my own father after that incident. It took me days to convince Daddy that I had not been responsible for it.

Vineet was holding Madhu's hands and consoling her right there in the restaurant. He seemed oblivious to the people around. I couldn't help thinking how good they looked together. Was there actually something going on between them now? I looked away, but then curiosity got the better of me and I simply had to steal a glance. I saw Vineet slightly brush her hair back and hold her close. She was crying into Vineet's arms. What was going on, I wondered. She did not want to have lunch with the others. That was clear. So, hadn't I better leave before Vineet felt it was like an obligation to be with me? I walked to them.

"Hey, I will meet you some other time then. You seem upset, Madhu. Vineet, you need to spend time with her." I was in no mood to walk away from the place. I was as upset as Madhu was. But I realized that then would not be the best time to talk to Vineet.

"Meera, I will talk to Vineet later. Sorry, you guys carry on." Madhu insisted that she joined the others. She wept inconsolably, bumping into a few people on her way to the table. That she was disturbed was beyond doubt, but the more disturbing part was that the man with me was growing distressed by the second as he watched her going away.

It was clear that Vineet wanted to be with Madhu. I made several attempts to let him know that it would be perfectly fine for him to join Madhu and Aman, but Vineet just stayed put.

"Why was Madhu so upset?" I asked Vineet.

"It is very sad, Meera. She was due for a promotion. The management had announced it to her, but the letter was withdrawn at the last moment. She feels that there is no point continuing in the office. She was fine a while back, but she just broke down upon coming here. I feel very bad for her. She has been working hard for this. She had spent days and nights in office working on a project that demanded a lot of time. This was just not called for. I will stand up for her. I am not going to let this issue die down so easily." Vineet was furious. It was clear that he was worried for Madhu. I could sympathize with her. After all, I had gone through something similar myself. I could not stop myself from wondering if Vineet would have been as worried for me as he was for Madhu. He had not been around at that time, but would it have been the same?

I caught Vineet looking at Madhu's table several times. I could not help feeling upset, but I decided not to be. I had no right to.

"What is it Meera?" Vineet finally asked me. "You were upset."

I had nothing to say. I was upset and I also realized that Vineet had moved on. He had other people in his life who were more important than I was. My feelings were no longer significant to him.

"Vineet. Is it ok if I call you and talk to you later? I am not feeling very comfortable. Sorry, that I asked you to come over, but I am not in the best of moods to talk to you now. Sorry again."

Vineet apologized to me for having got his friends along and offered to walk me home, but I refused. I waved to his friends and walked off.

I felt hot tears prick my eyes.

Vineet had moved on. I was no more a part of his life. Probably Madhu was going to fill in that vacuum. I saw him hold her with all the authority and love. I saw it all. Yes, they were going to be a couple soon. I have to be happy for him. No. I just didn't have to think about them. All my feelings were going with me to my grave. I did not want to share it with anyone. Nikki, *amma*, and others would laugh at me if I told them I could not stop thinking about Vineet. What the hell had I been thinking?

My phone rang just then and I picked it up all too eagerly. It was Malini from work and suddenly I knew what I had to do. I had to get back to work. Work was important now.

"Hi Malini. I am coming to work. I was going to call you anyway."

"No Meera. Work is all done. I thought that we should have a party. I have invited Drishti. Let us all meet at Dido at seven. My fiancé is coming as well. What say?"

Dido? Party? Memories from a time long past. I had sworn never to visit that place again.

"I will be there." I had to move on as well. I had to find a good life for myself. I was going to party.

BACK AT DIDO --- TO MOVE ON!

The party was unlike any other that I remembered. Somehow, I just did not seem to fit into the scene anymore. In the period since my last visit to Dido, I had undergone a thorough metamorphosis. However, the place itself had remained much the same. The bartender, for example, was the same and he smiled at me. But I could barely bring myself to smile back. The moment I walked into the place, a flood of hated memories involving Sanjay assaulted my mind. Was I destined to come back here just to relive those painful memories? I looked at the table and the bar stool in the corner at which Sanjay and I had sat that evening and a wave of disgust swept over me. How I wished I could go back in time and erase all those moments. I wished I could just wash off that one incident that had wrecked my life completely!

Malini and her fiancé were already there when I walked in. The couple seemed entirely at bliss in each other's company and so I let them be and concentrated entirely on waiting for Drishti. Twenty minutes later, when there was still no sign her, I resigned myself to the fact that Drishti had ditched me royally. Suddenly, I had this intense craving for company. One look at the cuddly couple at my table made me realize that no companionship would be forthcoming from that direction. Dido had reopened the wounds that Sanjay had inflicted. And the specter of the times with Vineet were also hovering over my conscience. It was like I had had a breakup. Well, technically, I had had one, but that had been months ago. So why was I suffering the aftermath now?

Dido may not offer me company, but it could offer me the next best thing – alcohol. I simply had to get high!

That evening, I drank until I dropped. Malini and her fiancé cheered every drink of mine.

"*Go on, Meera*", "*You are a rockstar*", "*One more, One more*"

Like a fool, I took their cheering to heart and downed five drinks one after the other. Malini tried her best to keep me company, but even in my inebriated state, I could see that she was caught in a tug of war between her friend and her fiancé and it was clear who was winning. I didn't really mind that all that much. The primary thought in my mind was that I had to move on. I had to get over Vineet by the time I was done with the party that night. Every drink was dedicated to the new principles of my life.

First – I was never going to feel guilty again

Second – I was going to move on

Third – I was going to forget Vineet

Fourth – I was going to forget Vineet

Fifth – I was going to forget Vineet.

I was high and I was miserable. The five drinks that had gone down were not helping me get over anything. Forgetting my earlier concern for their private time, I wrenched Malini from her fiancé's arms to pass on the critical information that I hated Dido. I also kept congratulating the couple on their engagement over and over again. I picked up my phone several times to call Vineet. I even dialed his number on a few occasions, but then quickly cut the call even before it rang. By the time I had downed my fifth, I had eight messages drafted to Vineet, but had not sent even one.

At one point, I took it on myself to point out to Malini how right her decision was. She was getting married to someone she loved and was doing it at the right time. Garnering all my accumulated wisdom and experience, I told her how critical it was to get the right feeling before taking the plunge. Malini, who was about as high as I was, nodded in agreement to all that I said. All the while, her fiancé was having a good time watching the two of us. I was just plain happy when he offered me a cigarette.

I took the cigarette and stared at it for a long time. My companions must have thought that I was attempting to smoke for the first time in my life and wondering which side of the stick to light! Not wanting to take a chance, the guy gently eased the cigarette from my hand.

In retrospect, that action of his is what, perhaps, saved the day for me. As I held the cigarette in my hand, my past and my present flashed before my eyes. I had a choice. I could simply light that cigarette and reopen the doors to my reckless, irresponsible past, or I could simply kick the butt and slam shut those doors for good. As the cigarette slipped from my fingers, I realized how close I had been to erring again. This was not the place I wanted to be. I had always regretted every drinking session that I had been a part of. So, quite literally, drinking was just not my cup of tea, glass of alcohol, or any other combination of drink and container.

After that, all I wanted to do was to leave the place. I was about to stagger out, when Malini requested me to take her to the washroom. She was clearly sloshed, dizzy and very miserable. It was clear that she'd need to be escorted to the bathroom. Together, the two of us walked towards our destination with unsteady steps, while her fiancé watched on with a concerned look on his face. Later, in a clearer state of mind, I'd reflect upon the irony of the fact that I, who could barely hold myself together, was helping someone else throw up. For the moment though, I was focusing on the poor thing choking and struggling to catch her breath.

Outside, Malini's worried fiancé waited, clutching her bag to his chest. Looking past him, I saw my own bag lying unattended on the table. Meera's belongings were of no concern to him! They were of no concern to anyone!

As Malini's conditioned worsened, I asked them to leave. I settled the bill and walked out to the lobby, remembering only then that I had no means of transport to go back home, other than a cab. The original idea had been for Malini and her fiancé to drop me home. But, as things turned out, I was left high and dry and with no option other than to fend for myself. I knew *acha* would throw a fit if he caught me arriving in a cab at that late hour. I could even then picture him pacing up and down the path that led from the gate to the house, fretting with worry. No, I decided, I couldn't take a cab.

"Vineet!"

"Hi Meera. What a surprise that you should call! I was just thinking of calling you."

"Really?" I asked

"Yeah, since we could not talk to each other today, I was wondering if we could make up for it tomorrow."

"Vineet, I am in a bit of a situation here."

"What happened?" he asked and I thought that a hint of concern was creeping into his voice.

"I had come out to Dido with friends and one of them fell sick. So the other had to take her home. He was supposed to drop me home, too, but couldn't. I am kind of stranded here, without transport. And, *acha* wouldn't want to see me come home in a cab or a rickshaw at this hour." I said.

"Are you alone, there?" Vineet was very worried.

"Yes. Could you come over? You are quite close to the place and so I called you. Can you come?" For a girl who thought a million times before asking someone for a favor, it felt strangely ok to be asking Vineet for help.

"Just wait inside. I will be there in fifteen minutes."

I heaved a sigh of relief. Though I had known exactly how Vineet would respond, there had been a tiny grain of doubt in my mind that he might have actually refused to come. I was starting to feel better already. While that was understandable, I couldn't help wonder why I was getting so excited at the prospect of seeing my ex-husband at that late hour! I could never have imagined feeling like this when we had been together. The misconceptions had given way to respect for Vineet, but the thrill that I was feeling was what was inexplicable. Suddenly there I was, drunk, stranded and absolutely smiling away to myself in that strange crowd. How would I ever thank Malini and her fiancé enough for abandoning me?

My phone rang. It was Vineet.

"Where are you, Meera? I just reached."

"I am coming out." I cut the call and raced to the door.

I saw Vineet's car right outside Dido. Though a tiny worm of embarrassment raised its head, I quickly crushed it, pulled open the door and climbed in. So eager was I to see him!

"What is wrong with you, Meera? When you loaf around like this do you even for a moment think about the people who care for you? Do you goddamn know what time it is! Eleven 'o'clock, Meera! People like your dad, mom, and I call it night…late night, even. Did you even bother to ask your friends to wait with you? What were you thinking? And you call them friends? You must be kidding!"

I sat frozen, with one hand on the door handle. But Vineet was just warming up.

"Do you remember that day you came home late? Do you even know how worried I was? But you don't bother about anyone right? Not even your parents. You are so self-centered. I was so pissed off that day for a long time. Maybe today is my chance to give you a piece of my mind. What if I had not been home today? There was actually a bright chance I would not have been, considering I was supposed to go out on a trek with Girish and Aman. You'd have had to take a cab home in that case, wouldn't you? Do you even read the newspapers? How many more brutalities against girls who travel home alone at night would you need to read before you come to your senses?"

I felt a lump rise in my throat. Vineet stared straight ahead with hard-set eyes.

"You just amaze me, Meera. You go out late in the evening and come back home at unearthly hours. You go out on an office trip and then drive back home in a colleague's car. You tell me that you guys drove together early morning. How am I supposed to feel about it, Meera? Why am I even bringing up the past? I don't care about those incidents anymore. But I had a feeling that you have changed, Meera. I am sorry to say you have not. Not in the least! You still go out at weird times with weird friends who don't care enough to see you home safe." Vineet was fuming. I had never seen him so angry.

I had expected Vineet Hariharan to pick me up, but this was someone else altogether. I mumbled an apology and stepped out. Though I viciously fought back my tears, they flowed out anyway. My fears, uncertainties and suspicions were all back again. I should have realized that the eagerness and anticipation that I had felt just a while ago was all going to be short-lived. It was a bad dream. As I walked away, trying hard to steady myself, I could hear Vineet calling me. But I was in no mood to go back.

"Meera, will you come back?" Still that angry voice.

"Vineet, please go home. Really sorry to have troubled you."

I was walking away as fast as I could, while fighting my tears at the same time. People on the road stood curiously watching the spectacle consisting of a man in a car, shadowing a lonely, weeping girl. I had so wanted to tell Vineet that all I had wanted to do was to speak my heart out. Not listen to any more tirades. But, I would have felt miserable had I broken down in front of someone who had come not to safely escort me home, but to vent his spleen for all the bad times from our past.

Vineet stopped his car at the curb and caught up with me.

"Meera, was I wrong in any way? I know that I no longer have the right to advise you. But is this how you react when someone points out your mistake?"

"You have always been right, Vineet. I have no complaints against you. It is my mistake. Let me go home. You go home too, please." I was averting my face.

"Stop!" I could sense his fury go up several notches in that command.

"Did you even understand what I was trying to tell you? Do you still think you are right? Stop. Will you please tell me? You were worried in the morning and then you walked off without even talking to me. And you think that simply stating that you were in no mood is explanation enough! You expect people to accept it without question! But if someone wants to point out a little mistake of yours, you just clam shut! How do you expect me to go in peace, leaving you to walk home all alone?" Vineet asked.

"What do you want me to do, Vineet? Ok, I'll admit this. When we met at uncle Swaminathan's, I realized how wrong I had been. I really thought I had seen all my mistakes and was actually happy that I could now begin going about setting it all right. Well, I now see what a fool I had been. My mistakes are not simple mistakes. They are blunders! Grave errors! I realize I have more than my fair share of shortcomings. I am a foolish girl, Vineet. I think I realize my mistakes but then go ahead and make them all over again. I am just wrong. Plain and simple. I have nothing more to say." I was wiping my tears. I tried to push Vineet away a number of times, but he wouldn't budge.

"Listen to me. I am angry, very angry at you. I was always angry at you. My parents disbelieved me and actually held me responsible for our break up. God knows how hard I tried to see the good in you all the while. But when you called me today, the cumulative effect of having held my temper in check all the time when we were together caused me to explode. You have been wrong Meera Madhav and it is high time that you actually realized that. Merely stating that you were wrong is not enough." Vineet held my arm in a vice-like grip to drive home his point. And, he was not done yet.

Vineet continued. "Both our families think that you were the 'good' person between the two of us. No one has ever made an attempt to understand me. My own parents branded me the 'wrong doer' without hesitation. Is that really the case? NO. I was never wrong in our marriage. You were responsible for it all but I was blamed always. You dragged me through hell and then let me face the music…all alone. While you were busy basking in your victories, I was going through hell trying to figure out what went wrong! You can't even begin to comprehend the number of sleepless nights and torturous days I spent trying tom find answers to the stinging questions. That morning, you just walked out on me declaring that the marriage was over. Did you even grant me a little time to come to terms with your decision? The rest of the world lost no time in looking down upon me with disgust, as if I was some ill-treating husband. Meera, give me one, just one instance where I was wrong."

I could not bring myself to look him in the eye. All I wanted to do was to leave the place as soon as I could, but Vineet retained that iron grip on my hand. It was evident that he was not going to let go of me without an explanation.

"I can only say that I'm sorry, Vineet." My voice was a barely audible whisper. For one instance, he looked me square in the eye and then let go off my arm in disgust. It was certainly the lousiest answer I could come up with, but, honestly, I had no other to offer.

I continued. "I was wrong. I had been judging you all the time. I deliberately chose to ignore all the extra efforts you took to make me feel good. I was busy making mistakes. You never earned a place in my heart. I hardly even thought of you as my own. You were so right about everyone and everything in my life. Sanjay, Bakshi, and Nexter were the biggest mistakes of my life. I hated it when you pointed out my mistakes. I refused to grant you any rights in my life, but was only too happy to hold you responsible for anything that went wrong at home. I disliked your friends and didn't think twice about behaving indifferently when they came home or when I met them outside. I was wrong. Vineet, I have been the wrong one between the two of us." It was with a growing sense of relief that I confessed to Vineet.

Vineet looked like he was going to say something, but I stopped him. I just had to open my heart out to him. "I wanted to meet you today to apologize to you. I wanted to confess to you about all the horribly bad things I had done in the past. You have every right to be angry with me. I know that I have humiliated you in front of your own family. I did not even care about your parents who have only ever been nice to me. They were very dear to me, yet I walked away hurting them. I was always there with my parents, never letting go a chance to tell them how wrong I had been. But, I understand how difficult things must have been for you. Sorry for being so insensitive."

I could no longer hold back my tears. I cried for a very long time. It must have been a sight for the few people still out on the streets. But neither of us were even bothered by it. Vineet had calmed down a bit by then. He probably had not expected that things would come to this. Usually, when a girl resorts to tears the guy meekly surrenders and lets the girl have her way. But my case was different. I could swear to god how hard I had tried not to breakdown before Vineet.

Vineet held my hand, saying in a soothing voice that it was

ok. I was tired of apologizing but I had to one last time. I held his hand and cried profusely. It was my way of letting him know what a great guy he was to be with.

We stayed in the car for a long time. Vineet had called *acha* up to let him know that he was dropping me home. After I had relaxed a bit, it was time for one last confession. "Vineet, there is something else that I want to tell you."

I was not sure if Vineet was inwardly bracing himself to face the consequences of the opening of yet another Pandora's box, but outwardly he retained his composure.

"Vineet, Sanjay and I...."

"I know, Meera. You don't have to say it." He held my hand and smiled serenely. He told me that he never wanted to hear about it.

Earlier, *acha* had surprised me by his calm reaction to my confession. And now here was another person who could have chosen to nail me to the cross if he so wished, but, who, instead, was choosing never to talk about it. I closed my eyes for a few seconds reflecting on my life and beginning to appreciate fully how wonderful it had been. I was not a perfect girl. Far from it. I was no example to set anyone to follow. But life had always given me another chance to make it right if not big. I had foolishly thrown away a great deal of happiness that had been offered me on a platter, but life was giving me another chance to correct my mistakes. It was perfect. I could not have asked for more.

Vineet started his car and slowly taxied out of the street. I turned to look one last time at Dido. As it receded into the distance, I knew in my heart that I had closed the door to my past forever.

"What are you going to tell your father?" Vineet smiled to me.

"I am going to tell him that he was right about Vineet Hariharan." I smiled back. As I opened the door, Vineet stopped me.

"Can we meet for lunch tomorrow?"

I smiled my most impish smile. "Only if Girish is joining us."

I walked away, happy. Something told me that good days were to come. It was not as if I was building any hope, because too much water had flown down the bridge. But it had been a day of relief. A day that relieved me of a guilt that had no business being there in the first place. It was a day when I had rekindled my life.

STAR-CROSSED

Vineet picked me up the next day for lunch. I had contemplated telling *acha* and *amma* that I was meeting him, but then thought better of it. I wasn't sure how to handle the million questions that were sure to follow. I felt like a teenager lying to her parents about going out with someone special. We went back to the same KFC. After all, there was a lunch to finish before the story progressed any further.

Girish and Reshma had joined us for lunch. This time it was Girish who pulled Reshma away to another table. He winked at me while doing so and I could not help smiling at him. Madhu had left for her hometown for a few days. I spoke to Madhu letting her know that I wanted to meet her once she was back in Bangalore. **Mukta** could definitely do with another partner.

I watched Vineet walk back to the table with our lunch. He was a special person. A special someone who knew my flaws, who bore my temper and above all who made me feel very special about myself. Fate had brought us together once again. We were back to being friends… Could we be more than friends?

"Ma'am, here's all that you ordered. Zinger burger, coke and Girish." Vineet and I looked at Girish with a smile. Since the guy was busy tucking into the largest burger on the menu, he didn't notice us.

"Thank you. Are you going to eat all of it?" I noticed that Vineet had ordered a lot of food. This could have been an influence of Girish's friendship, I thought.

"Do you have work today, Meera?"

"I do. Are you not going back as well?" I wondered why he was asking.

"No, I am in a good mood to bunk. If you remember, I had proposed this plan a long time ago. So, if I take half the day off, will you go out with me? And, please, we are not taking Girish along."

"Ahem. I am not really sure. I am not allowed to stay out very late, you see." I teased.

"Really? Do you turn into a pumpkin or something after twelve?"

It was the best lunch I had had in ages. We spoke and laughed easily about a million things.

"So," Vineet asked. "What are you going to tell your father today?"

"That Mr. Right was planning to bunk office today and abscond with his dear daughter."

Vineet chuckled and I thought it was the cutest thing I had ever seen.

Reshma and Girish joined us at our table. I invited them home and was genuinely pleased when they agreed to do so at the earliest possible opportunity.

"Meera, please ask your mom not to make anything special for me when I come home. As you can see, I'm on a diet." Girish was still chomping on a juicy chicken leg as he said this. I patted his arm in assurance.

When I turned back to Vineet, I saw him gazing into my eyes. The angry young man from the evening before was gone and in his place was this affectionate young man with the most earnest eyes ever. "Can we not give us another chance?"

I realized then how eagerly I had been waiting to hear those words.

"Should we?" I asked. "There is a lot that has happened. And our families?"

"Well, your family and mine think that we are a perfect pair. Remember all the stars, planets and constellations that were matched before." Vineet smiled.

I smiled back. "I disagree slightly. We are a star-crossed pair. A not-so-perfect match."

Vineet and I looked at each other disregarding the presence of our friends. He held out his hands.

There, in that busy KFC outlet, I took his hands in mine with a hope that it was forever.

Srishti's all time bestsellers ₹ 100 each

- A Dilli-Mumbai Love Story
- A Feeling Beyond Words
- A half baked love story
- A Life that you knew..
- A Little Bit of Love...
- A Little Love Incident
- And then it rained....
- Anyone Else but you
- A Roller Coaster Ride!
- As Long as I Love you...
- A thing beyond forever
- A Walk Down the Lane...
- Because you Loved me..
- Beep you! you BeepHole
- Belong
- Boundless Saga of Love
- By the River Pampa I...
- Careful what u Wish for
- Coming up on the show..
- Corporate Atyaachaar
- Crazy Bloody Thing LOV
- Dancing with Maharaja
- Everything you Desire
- Few things left unsaid

- From Cubicles 2 Cabins
- Heartbreaks & Dreams!
- I am Broke....! Love me
- I am Still Committed..
- If God Had A Desk Job..
- If God went to B-School
- If I Pretend I am Sorry!
- It Happened that Night
- In Course of True Love
- I too had a love story..
- It's all About Love...
- It Should Be u!! My Love
- It wasn't Love at First
- I will Love Once Again!
- Jab se you have loved me
- Journey of two Hearts
- Just Like in the Movies
- Life is What you Make it
- Love Happens Like that
- Love, Life & A Beer Can!
- Love, Life and Dream on
- Love, Life and Lust...
- Love Life & all the Dots
- Love, me and Bullshit!

- Love Power Politics!!
- Love a Rather Bad Idea
- Love & Urban Melodrama
- LUV is a Dirty Business
- My Love Never Faked...
- Nothing for you my Dear
- Nothing Lasts Forever
- Of Tattoos and Taboos!
- Oops! 'I' fell in Love!
- Ouch! that 'Hearts'..
- Patyala Down De Throat
- Plz.. Kiss me or Kill me
- Reality Bytes 'Bites'
- She is Single I'm Taken
- Simple Things Make LUV
- Something in your Eyes
- Sumthing of a Mocktale
- 34 Bubblegums and Candies
- That Kiss in the Rain..

- The Dev-D Syndrome...
- The Equation of my Love
- The Funda of Mix-ology
- The Idiot-Dudes.....
- The India I Dream of
- The Journey of Rock...
- The Journey to Nowhere
- The Lost Scraps of Love
- The Off-Site Tamasha
- The Other way Round
- The Quest for Nothing!
- The Thing Between U & Me
- Those Small Lil Things
- Three Times Loser....
- To Whom it May Concern:
- When Life Tricked me..
- What... if not I.I.T.?
- Will you Marry Me Cupid

- Brain Building for achievement
  Herbert N. Casson

- Cheiro's : Language of the Hand

- Winning Personality:
  The Magic key to success
  F. Oss